D1101462

FOOTSTEPS OF A STUART

Recent Titles by Elizabeth Elgin

ALL THE SWEET PROMISES
THE DAISY CHAIN SUMMER
WHERE THE BLUEBELLS CHIME
WHISPER ON THE WIND*
WINDFLOWER WEDDING

available from Severn House

FOOTSTEPS OF A STUART

Elizabeth Elgin

598162
MORAY COUNCIL
Department of Technical
& Leisure Services
F

This edition first published in Great Britain 1997 by
SEVERN HOUSE PUBLISHERS LTD of
9–15 High Street, Sutton, Surrey SM1 1DF.
Originally published in Great Britain by Robert Hale Ltd
under the pseudonym *Kate Kirby*.
This title first published in the USA 1997 by
SEVERN HOUSE PUBLISHERS INC., of
595 Madison Avenue, New York, NY 10022.

British Library Cataloguing in Publication Data

A record for this title is held at the British Library.

ISBN 0-7278-5299-X

All situations in this publication are fictitious and
any resemblance to living persons is purely coincidental.

Typeset by Palimpsest Book Production Limited,
Polmont, Stirlingshire, Scotland.
Printed and bound in Great Britain by
Hartnolls Ltd, Bodmin, Cornwall.

To Ruth Watters

ONE

THE NIGHT stole quietly from the hilltops and settled softly on Aldbridge. In the crofts that straddled the Green, cottagers slept and snored on mattresses of straw, and in her almshouse by the church, fat Goody Trewitt dreamed in her virgin bed of roasted chicken legs and strawberries and syllabub.

In the manor house that watched over the village like a wakeful mastiff, Sir Crispin Wakeman sat late in his armchair, the letter from Markenfield unopened on his knee. Now that his servants were in their beds, he would read the letter.

He trusted his servants, for they were all good Catholics, but the fewer who knew, the better. Ale could loosen a man's tongue, no matter how well its owner might guard it in sobriety. In an England ruled by Elizabeth Tudor, whom many held to be nothing better than a bastard usurper, Sir Crispin was but one of many Yorkshiremen who clung to the Catholic faith.

He was not prepared for the news the letter from Markenfield contained, and tears of joy fell unashamed on the stiff parchment.

" What is it, husband?" Anxiously Lady Hilda ran to his side. " Not bad news from Sir Thomas?"

" No, 'tis the best possible news he could have sent me. Our Queen is in England! Mary Stuart, our true Queen, has escaped from Lochleven and landed at Workington five days ago. She is now in safety at Carlisle."

Stiffly he fell to his knees and crossed himself.

The moonlight that silvered the May blossom and blessed the sleeping dead in the churchyard of St. Olaves, crept through the latticed glass of Father Sedgwick's bedchamber window and scattered his quilt with tiny crosses.

Father Sedgwick did not sleep. He expected a call to the corn-mill where Peter the Miller's mother lay dying. He wished the old woman would make haste about it. Twice he had given the Last Rites, and twice she had recovered. Now he would not move a step, he declared, until Peter heard the death rattle in his mother's throat. And for sure it would be heard tonight, when the priest's feather mattress enfolded him like a benediction, and Winifrede, his wife, lay quietly on his arm. Still-born babies and dying parishioners always needed a priest in the small cold hours. Why could they not die in the sunlight?

Father Sedgwick damned them all and turned his cheek to where Winifrede's black hair tumbled the pillow, and softly kissed the nape of her neck.

In the window of John Weaver's farm kitchen, a candle burned, and by its light Anne, his wife, counted her blessings as she polished her three new pewter plates.

But Meg, most loved of Anne's blessings struggled to free her ankles from the wooden jaws of the stocks into which they had been clasped.

"Thief! Thief! Gooseberry thief!" mocked the children of the village, as they danced round her.

"Stone her!" demanded strange voices. "Stone the thief!"

"Help me!" pleaded Meg. "Help me, Kit!"

She shielded her head with her arms, but Kit Wakeman stood silent on the edge of the jeering crowd, whilst gooseberries big as cobblestones hurtled through the air.

"Kit, they will kill me!"

Then hands were shaking her shoulders, and the dear familiar smell of her mother told Meg that she had been dreaming.

"Silly cuckoo," Anne stroked her daughter's hair. "What a caterwauling you make. You'll waken the dead with your noise! What ails my Meg?"

"Mother?" With a sob of relief Meg threw her arms round her mother's waist and felt her warm safe softness. "I dreamed they came and clapped me into the stocks, and strangers threw berries at me, big as rocks. And Kit would not help me. He stood there as they mocked me, and chanted that I was a gooseberry thief!"

Anne Weaver smoothed the pale soft hair that lay damp on her daughter's forehead.

"Silly dreamer. Go back to sleep. The sooner I take your precious berries and bake them into a pasty, the sooner we can eat them up and be done with them."

Then Anne kissed away the tears as she had always

A*

done, and pulled the blankets around her daughter's smooth white shoulders.

" Sleep well, my Meg. The angels guard you."

Anne returned to her hearthstone, her precious pewter forgotten.

Meg had always been a fanciful child, and nightmares and troubled dreams were no strangers to her. Always she called for her mother, and always Anne had been there to stroke her hair and kiss away her fears. But tonight Meg had called for Kit.

Anne frowned. Meg had not mentioned Kit when she returned from the tumbledown cottage with her pocket full of gooseberries. Young Kit must be home from school. He would be eighteen—a man, almost. It could well be, decided Anne that Kit's schooldays were over.

And what of Meg? Tonight, Anne must concede that her daughter was almost a woman. She must talk to Meg and explain that childhood was over. Girlish dreams and whims must be forgotten when a maid nears sixteen years. And with Meg's childhood must go her friendship with Kit, for he too was no longer a boy.

Kit was already pledged in marriage, and soon a husband must be found for Meg. Tomorrow Anne would speak to her husband about it, for with a mother's inborn instinct, she knew it could be delayed no longer.

That night, Kit Wakeman did not sleep. He did not think of the news he had brought from Markenfield Hall, startling though it was. He thought instead of Meg and and the gooseberries they had laughingly gathered. Kit had seen Meg by the ruined cottage as she bent over the prickly bushes, and had crept quietly behind her, placing his fingers over her eyes. He had not been prepared for the tremor that had shivered through her when their bodies touched. The last time he had seen her Meg had been just a girl—a sister, almost. He had never before noticed the blue of her eyes or the soft pale hair that flicked on to her shoulders—hair that today he had wanted to gently stroke.

It came as a shock to Kit that Meg was no longer a child. The play-fellow who trailed at his heels was gone. Meg was suddenly a woman, her breasts rounded and hard beneath the tight confines of her still childish dress. He had wanted to cradle those innocent breasts in his hands and feel again the quiver that would answer to his touch.

He wished Meg were a Catholic like himself. Most of all, he wished he were not pledged to Thomas Markenfield's dull daughter. Perhaps after all, it was not so good to grow up.

With a manly curse, Kit Wakeman pinched out the candle flame that burned by his bedside and closed his eyes against the tantalising moonlight.

The priest who brought the news from Workington, slipped silently over the moat-bridge of Markenfield Hall and made north to Norton Conyers. Catholic priests travelled warily in Elizabeth Tudor's England, the more so when the despatches they carried were treasonable. Sir Thomas Markenfield had rejoiced at the news, then made his confession and knelt with his family to hear Mass and receive the Sacrament before blessing the priest on his way into the night.

Already the news had travelled east to Aldbridge, and

before dawn it would be heard at Norton Conyers where lived Sir Richard Norton, and his seven lusty sons. Soon dale, moor and hilltop would throb with the news that Mary Stuart was in England and safe in Carlisle. Mary, whom many Northerners held to be the true Queen of England, and for whom many a man would gladly give his life.

And to the north of Norton Conyers, sitting on the edge of Redmire Moor, where the wild deer slept quiet in the May night, Castle Bolton waited, lonely and unknowing to play its part. Soon the far-reaching arms of intrigue would gather the silent fortress into the unfolding drama of the North. What would be the outcome none knew, save perhaps a lonely curlew. Its call piped sad and desolate that night over the moor, but none who heard it cared to heed its prophecy.

Stubbornly Anne Weaver resisted the fine new chimney stack.

" I see no need for it. And besides, it is wrong."

With patience nurtured by seventeen years of happy marriage, John stepped carefully from the ladder and laid his arm lovingly round his wife's shoulders.

" Wrong, love? I see nothing wrong in building a chimney for my wife, and Sir Crispin will see nothing wrong that I add well to his property. Will not your fire burn the better for a tall stack? Where is the wrong in it?"

" The stones you build it from. There is the wrong."

" But they are good stones, Anne, from the abbey. Stones that took me two days of labour to gather."

" Yes, stones from Fountains Abbey, placed there by the good Friars and dedicated to God. No good can come of sacrilege."

" Then by Our Lady, half the village is guilty of sacrilege, and King Harry too, God rest him! It was by his orders that Fountains Abbey was sacked. King Harry was head of our Church. Can *he* have been guilty of sacrilege?" Gently John cradled the troubled face in his hands. " If what I do it wrong, my Anne, and I am guilty of what you say, then guilty also was old Harry, and guilty now is Elizabeth, our Queen. A king and a queen can do no wrong. They answer only to God."

" And to their conscience, husband? Do they answer to their conscience? What of the Boleyn wench? Small protection her crown gave to her pretty neck!"

" Mistress Boleyn was mother to our Queen. You must not speak so. Were you not born on the same day as our Queen Elizabeth? And were you not named in honour of Anne, her mother?"

" I am not answerable for the actions of my parents that they named me so!"

The sweet May morning was becoming soured for John Weaver. He loved his thrifty wife beyond all reason. He was a happy man, who wanted nothing more than to work every daylight hour for the two people he loved best. A man of ambition who would soon have woven a pile of blankets high enough to trade for the fire-oven Anne had set her heart on. He did not wish to quarrel with his wife. He was sad that her conscience should trouble her over a pile of old stones, but he understood her uncertainty. Ann had been a serving maid to Sir Crispin's parents, and later to Sir Crispin and Lady Hilda. She had not adapted so easily to the new English church. It was reasonable she should have her doubts.

It was known that Sir Crispin would not attend prayers said in the English church, and paid his fine and those of his family and household each and every Sunday to Father Sedgwick. At the manor, morning prayers were said in Latin. Sir Crispin was only obeying his conscience as the Queen allowed. Provided a man obeyed his conscience in private, that was the end of the matter. There had been no burning of heretics when Elizabeth came to her kingdom. Elizabeth's hands were free from stain, which was more than could he said for Bloody Mary. John wanted Anne to understand this. It troubled him she should still have her doubts.

Taking her hands in his, John drew her down to the pile of stones.

" Sit with me, love. See, your holy stones do not bite our backsides. They are but stones. Give me a smile, and a kiss, and let me be about my business. Soon your chimney will be finished. Then we will light a fire in the hearth, and watch it glow red together."

But Anne was unhappy. Today, a fashionable new chimney stack meant little to her, and she sat with her husband's hand in hers, staring ahead and seeing nothing.

" What is the matter, Anne, love? Something troubles you. I know it by the way you brood."

" It is Meg—I worry about Meg."

" Is she sick?"

" She is sick, and she is not sick. I think Meg has thoughts of Kit Wakeman."

John laughed. " Meg has always had thoughts of Kit. They have lived within a stone's throw all their lives. They have been brother and sister almost."

" But brother and sister do not have thoughts of love. I think Meg feels differently now about Kit, although she does not realise it. I am a woman and I realise it. Meg has the love-sickness."

" Meg would not think so of one who is almost her brother," John said, unconvinced. " She knows it would be wrong. Besides, Kit is pledged."

" Aye, husband, and Meg too must be pledged. We should find a husband for our daughter, of good yeoman stock—and find him soon."

John jumped to his feet. " But Meg is only a child. She is scarcely sixteen. You were nearly twenty when *we* wed."

" I was nearly twenty because I had to wait for you to come out of your apprenticeship, because a stupid law says an apprentice may not marry until he has learned his craft. Not until you were twenty-four, John were you able to marry me."

" Has it been worth it, Anne? Are you glad you waited?"

" I am glad. I am a much blessed woman."

" Even though we lost our two sons?"

" It was God's will. He made Meg the more beautiful for it."

" Then keep Meg a child a little longer. It is only fashionable amongst the rich and landed gentry to marry so young. You and I, Anne, have no estates to split or to merge. We can afford to let Meg wait until she is ready."

" That we cannot, husband."

Anne had the bit between her teeth now. She intended to thrash the matter out, and John who knew and loved every mood of her conceded this.

" Meg can remain a child no longer, John. Perhaps her mind lags a little behind her body, but she has always been a dreamer. Meg is a woman, and must be treated as such. Your child is gone!"

" What must I do?" John said.

" I don't know. I spoke to Meg this very morning. Oh, she listened to me prettily, then skipped out of the door and over the wall. Doubtless she is now at the Manor with Kit, playing with the puppies, or some such childish game. She will not take my words seriously. Will you talk to her, John? Can you not make her see she must not love Kit Wakeman?"

" We will talk of the matter again." John could see the sense in what his wife had said, for Anne seldom argued unless she knew she was right. " We will talk seriously about Meg, that I promise you. But first let me be about my work, or I shall not finish my building in time to take you to market tomorrow."

Anne smiled and kissed her husband's cheek. The thoughts of a visit to the market at Knaresborough cheered her. There were preparations to be made for the journey, so she must idle no longer.

But Anne still thought about her daughter. Tomorrow in the market she would trade one of the oven blankets for fine linen cloth. Meg needed a new dress—a woman's dress. Now Anne sat in the sunlight at the open doorway, her needles clicking. As soon as the cap she knitted was finished, Meg must put her hair up as all women did. Once Meg did this, no man would see her hair about her shoulders again, unless that man were her husband. Perhaps when Meg put up her hair, some man would offer for her. The sooner the cap were finished, the better Anne would like it.

Meg was not playing with the deerhound puppies at Aldbridge Manor. She sat alone by the beck and thought about what her mother had said that morning. She knew she was growing up—she would be a simpleton if she did not know it. But did her mother have to make such a fuss and bother about it? She was glad about the new dress her mother had promised. It would not hold her tightly as the one she now wore held her. But put up her hair into a woollen cap—that she did not want to do!

She did not want to make it known, giggling as did the girls of the village, that she was in the market now for a man to wed. Better far to stand at the Hiring Fair like dairy-maids and house-maids and sewing-maids. There was no shame in *that*. But to put up her hair meant that a girl of yeoman stock was looking for offers, and Meg did not wish to think of a husband.

She would think instead of her new dress. Would it be made of silk, perhaps, from Florence? Or satin? Or velvet? Rich crimson velvet, patterned in gold with a ruff at the neck and a short shoulder cape? Would velvet be too hot for the summer? Satin, perchance? Blue satin, woven with silver thread, and dainty leather pumps to match?

Meg threw back her head and laughed. Her new dress would be made of linen, for sure. Plain and long-wearing, with a squared neck and tight-fitting sleeves. She would beg some fine threads and embroider the neck with flowers. Roses? No, not roses—for they would take too much time to sew, and besides, her mother had no red sewing thread. There was blue thread and yellow in her mother's sewing basket. Which flower was blue, or yellow? A violet or a sun-flower?

The answer was growing at Meg's feet. She shifted her toe and saw it—a clump of heartsease, their tiny blue and yellow faces turned up to her. She picked a flower and stroked the tiny velvet-soft petals. Pretty little heartsease—tiny wild pansies. She would embroider heartsease at the neck of her new linen dress—she would sew them there for Kit.

TWO

THE HAMBLEDON HILLS were far-away molehills and the weather was set fair. Only when those hills seemed to loose their feet from the earth and creep towards Aldbridge did the villagers know to expect rain. Today, John worked on his land, for this was a day for haymaking. The summer had been a good one, and now the July grass was thick and long and promised winter feed for his cow and young heifer. In a bad year John would have to kill his cattle and salt the beef, but this year the grass was lush, the corn grew green and sturdy and the root crop was thriving. This winter, none would go hungry in the Vale of York.

John moved steadily, his sickle swinging rhythmically in his right hand, his left arm scooping the cut grass as it fell and throwing it aside. And loaned for the day from Sir Crispin's estate, and working deftly towards John, came young Jeffrey. Tomorrow John would repay that day and help cut Sir Crispin's grass, whilst Anne and Meg worked their own field, turning and tossing the fallen grass, shaking and shifting it in the sunshine until it was dry as an old bone and ready to stack.

John paused and waved to Jeffrey to stop. Crossing the field with a jug of cider in her hand, and cheese and new-baked bread in a basket came Anne. John stood and watched her approach, her long dress swinging as she walked, her cap and apron white in the sunlight. In September, Anne would be thirty-five, and almost certainly past the years of child-bearing, yet as she walked towards him with a generous swinging stride, she was a girl again. A feeling of awe flooded through John.

He unwound the sweat-cloth from his neck and wiped his forehead and face. The cider in the jug would be cold from the slate and the bread crumbly and fresh. John smiled a long slow smile. Life was so immeasurably good that at times he feared the Fates would grow jealous.

There were no such notions in Anne's sensible head. She would never imagine the Fates to be jealous, for what Anne had, she and her husband had worked for. No one could deny them that. None could begrudge the new fire-oven, bought only yesterday in the market place in Knaresborough. Twelve blankets they had paid for it. Day upon day of teasing and carding the wool, of spinning until Anne's thumb and forefinger were ready to split, then winding the wool on to uncountable shuttles ready for her husband's weaving.

Anne would not for an instant think life could be jealous of her. She did not day-dream as Meg did, or feel cold fingers touch her spine. She was an earthy woman of York, sensible and solid as the grit and granite that made its foundations. And on that sunny day, she wanted nothing more than to bake pasties and meat in her new oven. She was so happy that had the Queen and her court walked through her farmhouse door, Anne would have conjured so fine a banquet from her fire-oven that even Elizabeth Tudor would have clapped her hands in delight.

John held out his hand as Anne approached, eager always for the closeness of her, taking the drinking horn she passed to him.

"What have you brought, Anne? A feast for a lord and his squire?"

"It is only cider, and cheese and bread. But what bread! It has baked so light it has doubled its size. Oh, John! I do thank you for my fine new oven. There is not an oven in the Riding to match it, save perhaps in Lady Hilda's kitchen."

She set down the basket with an excited laugh.

"Bread for my lord and his squire, scarce cold from the baking."

Gravely John took the flat bread-cake that was offered and broke it with his hands.

"Come Jeffrey, and sample the delights of the wonderful fire-oven. I'll swear you have never tasted the like."

The boy took the bread, then cut a slice from the cheese with his knife.

"I thank you, Mistress Weaver," he said shyly.

Anne's heart went out to the awkward boy as she watched him cross himself before eating his food. What a good husband he would make for Meg, come a couple of summers. Jeffrey was a Catholic as was his father, Peter the Miller, but Jeffrey would not inherit his father's corn-mill. A second-born of three sons must make his way by his own efforts. How good it would be, to take this likeable lad into her home and entrust to him the safe-keeping of her daughter. He had the same open honesty in his face that she had recognised in that of her husband and come to love more with the passing years.

Jeffrey would do well for Meg. Anne would speak to John about it that very night. When John's stomach had been well filled with roasted coney and strawberry pasty, that would be a good time to broach the matter of Meg's betrothal. When a man sits contented in his own inglenook, well cosseted and content, he would give his wife the fat yellow moon should she ask for it.

Anne turned and held up her hand in salute as she climbed the stone wall, smiling briefly at her husband's answering wave. She did not know why she had worried about Meg. The good God always provided in His own sweet time.

Slowly she walked home along the lane where dog roses tangled with honeysuckle and wondered what would greet her when she opened her kitchen door. Meg would sit there for sure, dreaming as she always did, the bellows idle at her feet and the fire grown cold under the bread cakes that were baking for Goody Trewitt.

With an impatient cluck, Anne quickened her step.

John was spared the agonising decision on his daughter's betrothing. That evening the clitter-clatter of a donkey's hooves and the roisterous greeting of Walter the Journeyman shattered Anne's carefully laid plans as surely as they shattered the pink-tinted dusk and stilled the evening song of the blackbird.

"What-ho, good friends! Are we welcome, my old donkey and me?"

With a shriek of delight and feet that scarcely touched the soft turf, Meg ran to the gate, her arms held wide in greeting.

"Mother! Father! Come quick. Walter is here," she called as she ran. "Walter and his donkey have come visiting!"

Then strong arms lifted Meg as though she were a puff of thistle seed and tossed her high in the air as they had done since she was a small child, and there was such a commotion of laughing and hugging and shaking of hands that Anne's tethered hens squawked and fluttered as though a fox were let loose amongst them.

"Walter, good friend. Well met!" John greeted. "Come into the houseplace. Truly you are more than welcome this night, for my Anne has need to show off her new fire-oven!"

His slow smile of pleasure gave strength to his words, for as always, even since they been apprenticed as boys to the Master-weaver in York's Felter Lane, John had never had Walter's gift of words or his early camaraderie. Their friendship had not ended with their apprenticeship, even though Walter had taken to the roads as a travelling weaver, and John had married his Anne. After twenty years the ties of their youth held fast as ever, with Walter never at a loss for a quick excuse to keep him foot-loose, and John, still the quiet one, content in his bonds of wedlock.

Such was the delight at the meeting of old friends and the giving of gifts—a copper skillet for Anne, and blue

ribbons for Meg, that none thought to question the early
arrival of Walter Skelton. Meg gave it not one thought as
she lay in the truckle bed of her early childhoood, her
knees pulled almost beneath her chin. It did not matter
that the bed was too small for comfort, for Walter was
dear to her and she made no protest when her own bed
was given to their guest.

Nor did Walter's untimely arrival unduly upset Anne's
thoughts as she lay in her bed that night, for already she
was making plans for the acquisition of another pewter
plate and a spoon and knife. It was wrong that their guest
should have to use his own wooden bowl and spoon.
But before Walter visited their house again, Anne vowed,
there would be a plate of fine pewter for him to eat off.

Even as her eyes closed drowsily, her thumb and spinning finger began to itch. Another blanket, and such
comforts would be hers to offer.

It was left to John to remark upon Walter's early
arrival as they sat together by the slow-dying fire.

"What brings you to these parts so soon? You do not
arrive in Aldbridge until the leaf-fall. Is work scarce that
you visit us so early?"

"No. Work is plentiful, even though Mary Tudor
harmed every weaver and wool-man when she lost Calais
for us," Walter said, and for once the journeyman was
serious. "Sometimes, friend, I envy you your pretty
little Meg, and Anne your wife. I'll swear there is no finer
cook as your Anne or a house so sweet and clean in all the
north country as the home she keeps for you."

Walter indicated the bunches of lavender flowers hanging on the walls of the houseplace and the fresh rushes on

the floor, plaited into mats and not strewn idly about and left to rot and stink with vermin.

"And you, John, had the good sense to rent this farmstead when the wool trade was bad. Now you have not only the trade of a weaver but you have stepped up the ladder to become a yeoman farmer. You sit contented by your fire with your belly filled with roasted coney and strawberry shortcake. You spin your wool and weave your cloth. Your rye and wheat give you bread, and your cows milk well to give you cheese and butter."

"What are you trying to tell me, Walter?" John asked slowly. "Do you think I am not aware of my good fortune? It is not too late for you to settle yourself in the ways of wedlock. It would make Anne happy to see you married to a good woman. Often she wishes it for you."

"Nay, John, I'll not be caught. Not even for a wife such as yours." Walter brought his great fist down hard on his knee, his serious mood gone. "No wench will coax me to the church door, not even if she has a fine chimney stack and a brass-handled oven for her dowry. Not if she bakes strawberry shortcake as good as your Anne bakes will I ever give up my freedom!" He gave a shout of laughter. "But it would be fine to be coaxed a little by such an angel. I'll swear I have not eaten so well since last I took my leave of you. Nor, come to think of it, have I supped such good old ale!"

With a wink, he held out his drinking horn to be refilled. But John was not deceived by his friend's sudden heartiness. He did not lift his eyes as he carefully poured ale from the jug by his side.

"Why *did* you come to us so early in the year?"

The question was simple and direct, and Walter knew he must answer truthfully, for John was too dear a friend to deceive.

"I'll tell you honestly, John, that I don't rightly know. Maybe it was the same instinct that bids an animal to seek shelter before a storm breaks, or that which hushes a songbird before thunder comes. You know that at this time I weave in Carlisle and then on to the house of the Apothecary, at Richmond, before I visit Aldbridge?"

John nodded. "I know that. It makes me ask why you are still not weaving in Carlisle?"

"Because I have no stomach for intrigue, good John. Because I am a simple weaver who travels from the Scottish border, south to York and then north again, according to the season, working for those who would hire my skills. I want no dealings with the rampagings of the Mosstroopers, on whichever side of the Border they ride. There is wild misrule in the Marches, with the Northern Earls strutting the hills as though they were kings and giving no mind to the laws of the land. Do you know they pay homage to the Scottish whore, and that Mass is being said openly on the English side of the Border? Would you believe me, John, if I told you that Mary Stuart holds court in Carlisle as though she were already crowned Queen of England? It was a sad day when Elizabeth Tudor gave sanctuary to the Scottish monarch—a woman accused by her own subjects of murder. Do you know of these things, my friend?"

"I know that Mary Stuart stands accused of knowledge of the murder of her husband, and that many Scottish

Protestants call her whore. But these things are not proven. What is there to fear from a frightened woman exiled from her own realm?"

" There is nothing to fear from such a woman, that I grant you." Walter Skelton drove his clenched fist into the palm of his hand with a rage that was strange to his easy nature. " But Mary Stuart is no frightened exile. She begs protection from her English cousin with one breath, then claims her protector's throne with the other. Already the Stuart has taken the arms of our Queen and tangled them with her own. She calls Elizabeth Tudor a bastard, and would have this kingdom if she could take it."

John Weaver said nothing—there was nothing to say. He felt again the fear that had chilled his happiness only that morning in the hayfield.

" But the Marches and Scotland are far away, Walter. Surely their ways do not concern us here in the Vale of York?"

" I'll grant you that it's safer in these parts than in Percy country, but what do you make of the strange happenings on Redmire??"

John shifted uneasily. The misdemeanours of the Percies and Nevilles in Northumberland and Westmorland could be of little harm to those who lived on the generous farmland twenty miles from the city of York and the Militia that was housed within its thick walls, well armed and always at the ready. But Redmire Moor was near at hand, a hunting ground for the local gentry.

" What do you know of Redmire, Walter? It is tavern gossip you would use to alarm me."

" I don't seek to alarm. To warn, maybe, but not to

alarm. I travelled from Carlisle to Richmond, and then on to Ripon by way of Redmire, and what I saw and heard there I did not like. First it was the carter with the strange singing voice of a man of the Tyne. He asked the where-about of Sir Crispin Wakeman."

John was slow to condemn. " But may not a man ask for directions without being accused of mischief?"

" Then tell me, John, why should he carry a load of sea-coal? Is Sir Crispin so rich a man that he can afford to have his coal carried overland? Is not all coal trans-ported from Newcastle by sea? What is wrong with Sir Crispin that he needs to use such foul black rubbish when the woods in these parts are rich with timber for burning? And why should the carter refuse my company when I offered to travel with him? The moors are lonely and wild. A man with nothing to hide should be glad of a fellow traveller."

" You make a mystery where there is none."

John fought the strange cold feeling that threatened to paralyse his reasoning. He knew Sir Crispin's chimneys were not built to burn sea-coal. Nevertheless, he made light of the situation.

" I fear you have drunk too well of Anne's best ale that you weave such tales."

" No, John. My brain is not fuddled, and what I tell you is God's truth. That Tyneside carter was a mite too inter-ested in Castle Bolton for my liking."

" But Castle Bolton is empty. It has not been lived in these five years."

" Castle Bolton is no longer empty, my friend. I followed the carter at a distance, intending to cross the moor behind him." He shrugged his shoulders, "I am afraid of no man, John, as well you know, but when I travel by night, it is only common sense to have a human soul within earshot. I tell you, that Northumberland man is no stranger to Redmire Moor. He travelled fast and I lost him in the darkness."

John threw a log on the fire. The room had become cold, and he was in no mood now for his bed.

"Tell me of Castle Bolton. I know of none who have lived there in recent years."

"Give me time to draw breath, and I'll come to that wretched place in my own sweet time." He set down his drinking horn, refusing more ale. "Nay, John, I'll drink no more of your brew yet a while, or you'll say my brain is befuddled, and you'll not believe one word I tell you. I caught up with the carter and his sea-coal. His horse was tethered and the cart pushed behind a screen of bushes and young trees. He was waiting and watching the comings and goings at the castle. There were lights in the windows and servants were carrying in furniture and hangings from where I know not. I tell you, John, it was all too secret for my liking. Then out of the dark strode a trooper, armed with a lance, and pulled me to my feet as if I were a common begger. 'What are you doing here?' he demanded of me. I told him I was a journeyman weaver, and was looking for lichens for my dyeing. 'Lichens for dyeing, is it? You gather lichens at nightfall?' 'Aye,' I replied, 'it is the secret of our trade that lichen gathered at night gives a stronger and deeper dye.' And do you know, John, the fool believed me and sent me about my business?"

A smile curved John's lips. "But you didn't go about your business, or I'm a Dutchman."

"That I did not. I returned and watched and waited like the Tyneside carter, and just before dawn I saw her arrive. Leastways, I think it was a lady. She was carried in a litter between two great black horses with troopers in attendance, and three women riding behind on horseback. And after them walked men and maids carrying packs, as though they were servants. It was a lady of some importance, or why did she need troopers to guard her? And why would such a retinue travel with her?"

"Do you think, Walter, that it was the Queen?" John Weaver's eyes shone with excitement. "Could it be that she visits these parts? Would you think it could be our Elizabeth?"

"Not for a minute would I think it could be Elizabeth. Would the Queen of England travel through the night like a fugitive? Would she rest at Castle Bolton, that cold, mildewed place, when she has a fine house of her own in York? Would not the whole county have heard of her coming? No, John, it was not Elizabeth Tudor the troopers were guarding, mark my words. Who she was I do not know. I know only that I felt evil in the air. There is something brewing in the North, and I'll feel safer when I have the stout walls of York to guard me."

That night when his guest had climbed the staircase to his bed, John stood at his door in the warm July night, the sleep his body craved evading him. Walter was right, thought John. There was evil afoot. He had felt it that morning and again that evening as they sat together in the firelight. His whole body tingled as he looked northwards towards Redmire Moor.

Slowly he walked to the rowan tree that grew by his gate—the tree all men planted who wished to guard their homes from evil. Touching the slim stem with the palms of his hands he whispered a prayer.

From witches and wizards and long-tailed buzzards
And creeping things that run in hedge bottoms
Good Lord deliver us.

Touching the cross of palm nailed to the door by Anne, he blessed himself.

" Sweet Jesus, guard this house and those in it from evil."

Bolting the door behind him, John took the string of lucky-stones that hung beside it and laid them in the hearth. Now no witch or evil power, clever as they may be, could enter John's home down his chimney. They dare not pass the lucky-stones.

Yet for all his safeguards, John did not sleep that night!

THREE

THE PINK-TINTED sunset that saw the arrival of Walter Skelton kept its promise of fine weather. Meg walked slowly across her father's hayfield, lifting and turning the fallen grass so that the sun might dry out the last traces of morning dew, listening as she walked to the drowsy humming of the bees and the tuneless chirping of swallows that dipped and swooped in search of insects.

It was work Meg liked—work she could do without effort, with nothing to interrupt her thoughts. Lost in her dreaming she did not see the rider who had tethered his horse and was walking towards her, for she was away in a world of magic in which the homespun dress she wore had become a gown of cool, flowing silk, and her thick knitted cap a garland of blossoms.

She almost cried out in alarm when from behind, hands closed over her eyes.

" Guess who I am ! "

" No need for guessing, Kit Wakeman," she laughed, dropping her pitchfork. " I saw you as you crossed the field."

" That you did not, for you were a thousand miles away, chasing your thoughts. Were you thinking of me, perhaps?"

" No, Kit, I was not. I was sitting in a dress of cool silk, dabbling my toes in an icy stream and watching this dratted cap as it floated away! I'll swear it's too hot to breathe!"

" Is my Meg at odds with the world this fine morning?" Kit gently chided.

" I am at odds with no one. I am hot, and this cap makes the back of my neck itch." She gave an angry toss of her head. " And I am not your Meg. That was made abundant plain to me this very morning."

" Sit with me in the cool of the trees, and take off your stupid cap. Then, my Meg, you will tell me what nonsense was so abundant plain this morning."

" I must turn this hay. My mother has left to prepare food for our guest, and I must hurry if I am to finish before she returns."

" I will help you finish," he offered. " I saw your mother leave the field, and I know that today your father works at the Manor with mine. I knew you would be alone. Tell me from where you dreamed up your nonsense, and why you have avoided me like a pestilence since I came home from my schooling. You *are* my Meg. You were always my Meg, and you will always be so."

Anxiously Meg looked towards the farmhouse.

" Kit, my mother will rant if she finds you here. I must not meet you again. That my mother ordered."

Arrogantly the boy took the fork discarded by Anne, and started to toss the hay.

B

" The sooner we finish, the sooner we can rest in the shade."

Some time later, Meg shook off her pumps and wriggled her toes in the grass that grew green-cool beneath the trees of the wood.

" Lord, Kit, 'tis too hot to breathe."

She lay on her back and looked upwards to where the thick foliage of the oaks shut out the sunlight. The earth was cold beneath her body and she closed her eyes and sighed with contentment.

" I'll swear yon field is hot as Lucifer's cauldron. Kit?" Meg opened her eyes. " Why do you not answer me?"

Lying beside her, arm crooked, hand beneath his chin, Kit smiled.

" Is it indeed, mistress, as hot as Lucifer's cauldron?" he replied with laughter in his eyes.

" You tease me. I'll not be teased!"

Meg pushed Kit's elbow so that his arm slipped and sprawled over her body, his face hitting the grass near her own with a soft thud. He lay still, his eyes closed.

Meg struggled to sit up, but Kit's arm lay across her like a dead weight, and she could not move.

" Kit? I've hurt you?" she said, shaking his shoulder with her free hand. " Kit, love, speak to your Meg."

Suddenly Kit's arms were round her and for a moment his eyes were laughing into hers. She opened her mouth to protest and in that instant the laughter left his eyes, and playful chiding words seemed wrong and stayed unspoken. Slowly Kit's fingers touched Meg's cheek and traced the outline of her lips as though forbidding her to speak.

Gently he reached for her cap and with a movement of her head that said " No ", Meg's child-soft hair fell to her shoulders and scattered the grass like the unwoven threads of cloth-of-gold.

" So you *are* my Meg?" He spoke the words slowly, challengingly, daring her to deny him.

Meg lay still, her eyes not leaving Kit's, her whole body aware of his nearness. She had felt his closeness before, and she had been unsure of her feelings. Now his arms around her felt right and real and she wanted to lie there for ever in the soft enchantment of the wood.

This morning her mother had told her she was growing up. Was this then growing up? Why had her mother not told her of the feelings of being a woman—of the strange surging inside her? Meg knew with sudden sureness that the boy in whose arms she lay was hers to command. Instinctively she knew that a turn of her head, a lift of her shoulders, or the soft brushing of her lips on his closed eyelids could make him into clay in her hands to mould and manipulate as she willed.

" Yes, I am your Meg," she spoke the words softly, " and you are my Kit. And always will be."

She touched his hair and with the tip of her finger, followed the arch of his brow, seeing his face for the first time with the eyes of a woman. The strangeness she felt was gone and a triumph was singing inside her that wanted to burst out like the surge of water in a mill-race. Meg knew now the power that was Eve's and it was heady as wine.

She closed her eyes and slowly tilted her chin so that her mouth was close to Kit's. Her lips parted to receive his kiss and in that first moment of their love, the singing inside her exploded into a thousand shooting stars and the beating of her heart thundered an ecstatic warning in her ears.

She felt a lightness in her body as though she were being borne along on the crest of a foaming wave and at the same time drowning in a bottomless sea of feather-down. She wanted to abandon herself to the wave and go with it wherever it would carry her, yet within herself she struggled against the engulfing softness that was slowly suffocating her mind and sapping her will.

With all the strength inside her, Meg flung herself free of Kit's arms, rolling her body away from his before she scrambled to her feet.

" No, Kit, no!" the cry was half entreaty, half command. " It is wrong! Let me be, Kit."

Swaying dizzily, she tried to quiet the pulses that throbbed at her throat and in her breasts. She stood like a cornered deer, not knowing whether to fight or to run, certain that either was hopeless.

" Lord's sake, Meg, what is this?" Kit was on his feet, and reaching out for her. " First you invite me, and then you repel me. What woman's game do you play?"

They faced each other, an arm's length apart, tense as animals waiting to spring.

" I play no game, Kit. I remembered that you are pledged, and that this morning my mother told me I must marry Jeffrey."

" Marry Jeffrey? He's a yokel."

" Jeffrey is no yokel, but I do not wish to marry him."

"Nor, Meg, do I wish to wed Markenfield's daughter. Besides, the dowry has not been settled and the marriage bond is not signed."

"Signed or not, Kit, you will marry her as I shall marry Jeffrey. We must do as our parents bid."

"It is *you* I want. I have always wanted you, yet today is the first time I have really known it. I'll have *you*, Meg, or I'll wed no one, that I swear!"

"You'll wed the Markenfield wench and her dowry. Old Sedgwick will tie the knot and then you'll be blessed again in secret by a priest of your own calling. You'll be doubly wed, Kit."

The hopeless little shrug of Meg's shoulders touched Kit's heart so that he wanted to hold her again in his arms. At that moment in time he would have fought the world for her.

"Meg, dear love, I care nothing for Markenfield's dowry. I am my father's only child and will inherit all that is his. I have no need for marriage gold. I will tell my father about us. They cannot make me marry nor carry me protesting to the priest!" Gently he kissed her mouth. "If only you would worship in the true faith, Meg, and not listen to the false cant of Elizabeth Tudor's priests, I know I could persuade my father to accept our marriage. You know that secretly my family does not acknowledge Elizabeth Tudor to be the Head of our Church?"

"I know. It's one of the best known secrets in the Riding. And speak not so of our Queen, Kit. She is lenient to all men. Be thankful you can hear your Mass and that Elizabeth Tudor turns a deaf ear to Latin chantings. Catholic Mary and her Spaniard did not show such charity to those who professed the Anglican faith, I know that much from my father."

" And what, sweet Meg, did your mother tell you? Cannot you listen to your mother's teachings? Is not your mother still of the old faith, even though she worships in the English church?"

Meg shook her head in bewilderment. " I don't know, Kit. At night my mother prays in English, then says her Rosary to make doubly sure the good God has heard her. My mother is as confused as you seek to make me."

Gently Kit cupped Meg's face in his hands.

" Little bird, I do not seek to confuse you. If only you could profess the true faith, I know there would be no obstacle to our marriage. Let me speak first with my father. He is a good man and will hear me out."

" Your father would not give his blessings to our marriage, Kit, even if I were of your faith," Meg reasoned gently. She was younger than Kit by two years, yet now there was a wisdom about her that belied it. " I come from yeoman stock, and you, Kit, are of noble birth. It is wrong that we seek to marry out of our station. We are as we are born. We cannot change it."

" Then run away with me, Meg. We'll be married in secret. Once the priest has tied the knot, there'll be no untying it."

" The knot of an Anglican priest, Kit? How could such a priest set the seal on the marriage of a Catholic? Would you take me in sin then, for mortal sin it would be in your eyes!"

" Not if our marriage was blessed by a true priest." Kit held out his arms. " Tell me that we shall be wed

before another sundown. Say you will come with me to
Ripon. I know where to find a priest of my faith there
who can marry us."

Meg backed away. If Kit should touch her again the
wave would toss her once more to the giddy heights of
madness, and she would be lost.

" No, Kit. What you would do is wrong. You know it as
well as I. Our love would die slowly and surely when
deceit entered into it."

A sob rose in her throat as she spoke—a cry for the
child that was gone, and for the woman she had become.
Suddenly the world about her was a vast and frightening
place. She could no longer run to the comfort of her
mother's knee or the gentle strength of her father's
protective arms. On this day she had grown up and the
arms she longed to feel about her she knew she could
never have. Emotion raged inside her and tore at her heart.

She turned to Kit, her eyes blazing passion, her words
incoherent and tearful.

" God's Life, I can find it in me to damn all religion
and man-made mockeries that keep us apart! Should it
matter that I am beneath you in station? Is it wrong that
the beliefs of our religions should serve as a wall between
us? There is only one God, Kit, and one Hereafter. What
does it matter if we pray in our native tongue, or in the
Latin of a foreign Pope? Shall we never meet again after
death because you think me a heretic or because the
Queen will not bend her knee to your Pope?"

Chastened, Kit stood helpless and mute. This was a
Meg he had never seen before. Here was a woman whose
fire matched his own. And this woman he vowed he would

have, with or without the blessing of any church.

" Kit, my love."

Meg held out her arms and together they sank to the moss-made carpet of the wood. Gently she stroked his forehead and smoothed his unruly hair. Tenderly she kissed his cheek, all passion gone.

" Kit, sweetheart, is there somewhere a world into which we can be born afresh after we have died? Some place where the souls of all people, be they Catholic or Protestant, Anglican or Infidel, can be born anew in some other form? Shall we two come to this earth again as birds, and fly together into the sun? Or shall I perhaps be a flower and you a honey bee that kisses my petals and drinks of my soul? Shall I die, Kit, and grow again as this tiny pansy grows at your feet? And will you pick me and hold me to your heart? Shall I be your heartsease, Kit?"

There was a moment of quiet between them.

" You think we can come again to this earth and find each other in some other life?" Kit said slowly. " Do you truly believe we can take another form?"

" I don't know, Kit, I don't know. I think I would believe anything that would give me comfort. If our souls can fly to our Maker when we die, why cannot they enter into another form? It is the only salvation we can hope for, you and I. Shall I die of a broken heart and come again to you as this pretty little heartsease?"

She picked the tiny wild pansy growing at Kit's feet. Lovingly she offered it to him. " One day in such a flower you will find my soul, that I promise you."

But Kit did not take the flower Meg offered. What had

been the sweet talk of lovers now suddenly became abhorrent to him.

"You say we can enter into another form and of our own free will?" Disbelieving, his eyes sought hers. "Tell me you only jest, Meg, for what you say is heresy—nay, worse! Such talk is devil's talk. 'Tis witchcraft!" The words were a horrified whisper. Hastily he blessed himself. "Say you were joking, Meg, for you know as well as I that only a witch can take another form. Tell me you meant only to tease."

"You have known me since I can ever remember. Do you think your Meg who loves you is a witch? Do you, Kit?" She took his chin in her hand and tilted it so that he was forced to look into her eyes. "Tell me, is it a witch who loves you? Do you see a witch before you?"

"I see the woman I love, and I know she is a dreamer." Kit took her hand and held it between his own. "Swear on our love and on God's Holy Blood that you will never speak so again. There are some who would believe your silly rantings, for they do not know you as I know you. Swear to me, Meg, that what you said was only a joke."

"Dear heart." The sight of his anxious face touched her. She loved him too much to deny him anything. "On our love, I swear. Forgive your Meg for loving you so much that she would say such things." She gave a little sigh, and smiled up at him. "But when you have married the Markenfield wench, remember this day, Kit. Remember it and never step upon a heartsease, lest you wound your Meg."

Kit's protest died on his lips as a shadow fell between them. Together they looked up.

B*

" So, Meg! Is this how you turn the hay? And you, Master Kit, be about your business before I box your ears soundly. Why a grown man like yourself is not working in his father's fields I do not know."

Anne looked down on the young lovers. From a distance she had seen them sink to the ground and her lungs had fairly burst with running. They had not seen her as she hurried towards them, so engrossed were they one with the other.

" On your feet, miss, and pick up your cap. Do you romp in the woodland like a common strumpet? I'll swear I'll take a birch rod to you, big as you are!"

Anne's anger was plain to see. The cider she carried in her jug had spilled out as she ran across the field and her face was flushed with exertion and indignation, despite her relief that no damage appeared to have been done.

" Be on your way, Kit Wakeman, or I'll speak to your father about your behaviour. Drat you that you seek to spoil a young maid!"

Since time began, there has been no fury like an angry mother, and this Kit knew. Sullenly he dusted down his jerkin and pulled on his gloves. A few moments ago he would have fought all creation for his Meg, but now he must slink away, whipped like a puppy by Mistress Weaver's tongue.

Deliberately he avoided Meg's eyes. There would be other times and other places. He would have Meg, that he silently vowed. Flinging himself on to his horse he jerked the reins viciously and jabbed at his horse's flanks with the heels of his boots. The devil take Mistress Weaver and her interfering.

The devil take his father too, for making an errand boy of him. He might have known there would be an urgent letter to carry. Whenever the Northumberland carter arrived in the night with his sea-coal there came the need to ride with news to Sir Thomas at Markenfield Hall. There had been such rejoicing last night that they had almost forgotten to unload the coal and hide the swords and pikes that were hidden beneath it.

Kit wondered if Sir Thomas Markenfield had yet heard the news. What a surprise it would be to him, and how important the bearer of such news would appear in the eyes of his daughter, Amy. Perhaps when he had delivered the letter, thought Kit, he would ride over Redmire Moor to Castle Bolton. Perhaps he would see her there. He had never seen a queen before. How wonderful to fall on his knees at her feet and pledge his life to the cause of the true Queen, for in the eyes of God and Kit Wakeman, Mary Stuart was England's true Queen. And the sooner she ruled England the better, for then Mass would be said again in all the churches, and Meg would be a Catholic and they could marry.

The air shimmered golden in the heat of noon as Kit Wakeman set his horse's head towards Markenfield. The sun was hot on his head, and he wished he had remembered to wear his fine new hat. It gave him a rakish air and would have impressed Amy Markenfield. But no matter! The day was fair. There was intrigue in the air, and maids for kissing and maids for wooing. Kit laughed out loud, his encounter with Meg's mother forgotten. Life was for living. And life was good!

FOUR

IT HAD been no trouble, thought Kit, to bribe the carter. Only a few sly glances, a whispered confidence that he wished to see the pretty serving wench who worked in the kitchens, and a gold crown, were all that was needed to gain his admittance to Castle Bolton. If it proved as easy to set free the Queen as it had been to enter the stronghold, Mary Stuart was as good as on the English throne.

" Take this pack, young sir, and walk behind me," the man had said, pocketing the crown. " When we get through the big gate, the kitchens are on your right hand. After that, it's up to you." He grinned, as he hoisted a bundle of bedding on to Kit's back.

A thrill of excitement shivered down Kit Wakeman's spine and tingled along his arms to the tips of his fingers. Before him stood the squat and angular building that was Mary Stuart's prison. The rest of the day now counted for nothing; not the tumbling with Meg in the cool of the wood, nor Anne Weaver's angry tongue, nor yet the cow-like gaze of adoration with which the Markenfield wench had looked upon the bearer of important news such as Kit had carried.

It was as well his father's mind was occupied with other things, Kit decided, or Amy Markenfield's dowry would have long been paid and the marriage bond signed, and before he'd known it, he'd have been heading for the church porch and indissoluble wedlock. Instead of which, he had just bribed the carter who carried hangings and bedding from the nearby home of Sir George Bowes, for hastily furnishing the castle that had stood empty these last five years.

It was wrong, mused Kit, that a Queen should be treated so. And in her own kingdom, too. For England was Mary Stuart's lawful realm in the eyes of all those who clung to the old faith. Catholics could not acknowledge the marriage of Old Harry Tudor to the Bullen witch. Elizabeth, their child, was a bastard, and the only true Queen of England was Mary Stuart, already Queen of Scotland, and Queen Dowager of France.

But soon that great injustice would be righted, for the loyal catholics in the North would overthrow the usurper and install the rightful Queen at Westminster. More important still, the heretic priests would be scattered and Mass would be said again in all the churches. Soon, thought Kit, when the church bells sounded a tocsin of peals rung backwards, the faithful would know to rise and arm themselves, for God and Mary Stuart.

" Psst! Over yonder, young master," hissed the carter, relieving Kit of his pack. " Your head was in the clouds. Good hunting, my fine young blade, and watch out for the troopers, for if you are caught, I'll swear I've never clapped eyes on you before!"

" I'll not get caught," Kit boasted with a grin, walking

in the direction of the carter's pointing finger. But he would never know how pretty the serving maid was! Or even if she existed at all!

The carter had told Kit that a nobleman from London had arrived at Bolton in the early morning, hot on the heels of the lady who travelled through the night.

" They say," the man had confided, " that he is a gentleman of importance and related by marriage to Queen Elizabeth. You are of noble birth, young sir. Maybe you will know him. I was told his name is Knollys."

Kit knew of Sir Francis Knollys. So, the sanctimonius old Puritan was to be Queen Mary's jailer. Kit suppressed a laugh. No doubt his lady wife would be glad to see the back of him for a few months, if only to avoid another of her frequent pregnancies. They said Sir Francis had more arrows in his quiver than he could count! A fig for Puritan piety, thought Kit, as he walked across the courtyard, unnoticed and unchallenged. With luck he would find the rooms of Mary Stuart. Without it, he would land up in Sir Francis Knollys's bed-chamber.

Drawing a deep breath, and whispering a prayer to St. Olave, Kit made for a door set in the wall by a flight of stone steps and cautiously opened it.

After the heat of the day the stone passage was pleasantly cool and Kit blinked his eyes in the un-accustomed dimness. The little gasp of fear startled him, for he had not expected to encounter anyone so soon.

" Who are you, sir?" It was a woman's voice, cultured, but with a strange lilting accent. " What is your business?"

" I am Kit Wakeman, of the manor house at Aldbridge."

It was foolish of him he knew to give his real name but

the woman had caught him off his guard. Now, as his eyes became accustomed to the darkness of the passage, Kit could see she was of noble breeding.

" Then go home to your manor house, Master Wakeman, unless you have business with Sir Francis Knollys."

" Nay, not with *him*."

The swiftness of Kit's answer made the woman look at him strangely.

" Then who, sir, do you seek?" she asked slowly and meaningly.

" I seek one who is lately come from Carlisle," Kit hazarded.

The woman caught her breath. " How did you know of our journey from Carlisle?"

Kit shrugged his shoulders. " Queen Mary has many friends in the county of York."

With a gasp of relief the woman took Kit's hand in hers.

" Come quickly, young sir, and I will find a place where we can talk. I feared you had come to harm my mistress."

" Never that, Madam. The people in these parts are loyal to the old faith. We would like to see our true Queen on the throne of England. One day, mistress, with God's help, she will claim what is her birthright."

The small woman with the soft voice drew Kit into an alcove.

" I am Mary Seton, young sir, lady-in-waiting to Queen Mary of Scotland. If you come in peace, you are truly welcome, though what will become of you or me if we are caught, I know not."

Kit raised the woman's hand in his and raised it to his lips as he had heard was the practice in the French courts. Doubtless, Mistress Seton would know all about the gallant ways of Frenchmen.

" I come in peace, Madam, with my life as a gift to her majesty. I had foolishly hoped I might catch a glimpse of her, or even assure her of my loyalty. But I am well met with you, Mistress Seton. Will you tell Queen Mary that there are many here who love her and who are pledged to see her in her rightful position?"

" Seton is not here to run messages for younglings. Tell the Queen yourself, boy."

Silhouetted in the open doorway with a narrow window behind her, the woman gave a little laugh.

" Well, boy, where is the tongue that waxed so eloquent half a minute ago? Has the cat run off with it?"

Kit dropped to his knees, his hands clasped tightly, eyes glued to the ground.

" Your Grace," he whispered, his voice rough with emotion.

" Madame, I beseech you, it is not private here . . ." anxiously the lady-in-waiting pleaded. " It is better to withdraw and close the door behind us. We are not yet sure who are our friends in this awful place. We may be seen, and this youth would come to harm."

" You are right, Seton." Mary Stuart walked into the room. " You are always right, and I would not harm one curl of this young gentleman's fine red hair!"

Kit rose to his feet, his awe forgotten.

" Madam, I care not for my locks. I came to swear allegiance to my Queen, and I lay my life at her feet."

Kit looked at the face before him. It came as a shock to him that Mary Stuart was exquisitely lovely. Her skin glowed white and her nose was straight and finely moulded. But most beautiful of all her amber eyes—perhaps a legacy from her Tudor grandmother—were slanted beneath her finely arched brows like two glowing almonds. She was tall, too; taller than most women Kit had seen.

"Why do you stare at me? What is amiss that you gawp so? Is it my hair? Do you find it offensive?"

"You are so beautiful, Your Grace." Taken aback, Kit could only stammer out the words.

"I am sorry, boy, that I spoke so. I am nervous and tired, still, from my long journey. Forgive me if I am vain about my hair. This black topping is not my own. My own hair was sacrificed when I fled my prison in Lochleven. I sliced it off in great haste so that I should look like a serving woman, and I must hide my poor efforts at barbering with this hair piece."

Mary Stuart was instantly contrite, and Kit loved her for it.

"Once in my youth that seems so very long ago, my hair flamed golden like yours, boy. We are all alike who have red in our tresses. We are impulsive, and do not think before we speak."

"Nay, Madam, do not deride yourself so, for in my eyes you are perfection."

Mary gave a little laugh at the youthful compliment. It was good to hear her laugh, thought Mistress Seton. Perhaps the young gallant spoke the truth. Maybe soon her mistress would once more rule like a queen.

"I had doubts when I left my own country." Mary picked up her embroidery frame. "I could not be sure that I was right to come to England and throw myself upon the mercy of Elizabeth Tudor. At times I felt it would have been more fitting if I had sought sanctuary in France. Now, suddenly, you bring me hope. I think Elizabeth Tudor will help me regain my throne. She is my kinswoman and a queen like myself. She will not fail me."

"Your Majesty, do not trust the word of the Bastard. She will not help you. She sits on a throne which is not rightly hers, and she will keep you a prisoner here," Kit was quick to protest.

"Nay, young sir, I am no prisoner. I came to England of my own free choice. Elizabeth will help me crush the rebels in my own country. A court will soon sit at York to prove that I am innocent of the charges my half-brother throws at me from Edinburgh. Soon it will be proved that I had no hand in the killing of my husband. Then Elizabeth Tudor will aid me. I know it."

Kit opened his mouth to speak. *I'd as leave trust a hungry wolf*, he was about to say, but thought better of it. Mary Stuart trusted Elizabeth Tudor, of that he was certain. The poor misguided creature really believed that with her cousin's aid she would regain her Scottish kingdom. Couldn't she see, the sweet innocent, that Elizabeth Tudor would do no such thing?

"It is the least she can do, Madam, considering she sits upon Your Grace's English throne!"

Kit could not believe a woman could be so utterly without guile. Surely Mary Stuart could not think she was a free woman? All seemed well on the surface, but let her try to walk one step in the direction of freedom and she would soon know she was at Elizabeth Tudor's mercy.

Already it was reputed the Queen of England was wearing Mary Stuart's fine pearls, and sold to her by the Earl of Moray, Mary's half-brother.

"Nay, boy, do not speak so of the Queen," Mary was quick to spring to Elizabeth Tudor's defence. "I do not like to hear it, for what you say is treason—I say this to you as I would say it to my own son, were he with me. Did you know, boy, I have a son? He is but a baby, yet I still miss him sorely. One day, perhaps, I shall have him with me."

Her eyes took on a far-away look, as though they were searching beyond the hills of the Palace of Holyrood where he lived, and her eyes filled with tears.

"Your Grace, do not distress yourself."

Kit was so overcome that he would have torn out his heart for her, without a moment's hesitation. The sooner this gentle creature were Queen of England, the better it would be for all.

"Your Grace, only tell me what I can do to aid you, and it will be done." Kit dropped to his knees again. "There must be something. Take my right hand," he offered in desperation. "Take my heart—it is yours anyway."

"Stand up, youngling," smiled Mary Stuart. "Stand up tall, for there *is* something you can do for me. I wish to write a letter to a friend who is anxious for news of me. Could you get it to the Earl of Northumberland for me? He will deliver it to its owner."

"That I can, Majesty. The Earl has a house at Topcliffe, and I know it well. I will give it to his steward, who is loyal also to your Grace."

The Queen of Scotland rose from her chair and dropped her sewing on the table beside her.

" You may sit and take a sweetmeat from yonder box, boy, and I will write to my friend."

" Make haste, Madam," anxiously Mary Seton hovered. " It is nigh on suppertime, and I fear what will happen if we are all caught."

The Queen gave a happy little laugh. " We will not be discovered, Seton. God protects the Right. Willy Douglas shall smuggle the youngling safely out of this place. Do not fret, Seton. Do not fret."

Kit walked over to the window set high in the tower. On all sides rolled hill and moorland, now quietly darkly green in the late day sun. For miles around, almost as far as he could see, there was no human habitation, no friendly soul within earshot, if he discounted Mary Seton. All those employed at the castle must surely be in the pay of Cecil, or Knollys.

In the courtyard there had been troopers. Surely Queen Mary had seen them. Could she, good though she was, ever imagine they were her friends? Kit's blood boiled for the beautiful and wronged woman who sat, head bent with a smile on her face, writing as though her life depended upon it. Was she perhaps, enquiring for news of her baby son? A lump rose in Kit's throat. He had been true to Mary's cause long before he had met her. Now, he silently vowed, he would not rest alive until she rode in triumph through the streets of London to her crowning.

The sun was setting before the letter the Queen of Scotland laboriously wrote, was finished.

"All is well, now," she smiled captivatingly at Kit. "Hide behind the hanging, boy, in case the serving maid should enter with our food. As soon as it is dark, Willy Douglas will steal you out of this place, and you shall deliver my letter for me. I would withdraw now, to my bed, for I am tired still with so much travelling."

She held out her hand to Kit, who took it and kissed it almost reverently.

"We are indebted to you, sir," she said.

Later that night Kit Wakeman rode slowly home, a feeling of elation keeping him wide awake, even though it was long past midnight. It would be sun-up before he sighted Aldbridge again, but he did not care. Nor was he afraid for his safety on the desolate wastes of the moor. Nothing that lived or breathed could harm him now, for he was Mary Stuart's sworn man. His life was hers. The beautiful creature had captivated him utterly.

In the bed-chamber at Castle Bolton, Mary Seton brushed her mistress's hair, then kneaded her fingers against the royal scalp.

"The rubbing will aid its growth, Madam," she said. "Soon your hair will be long and shining once more."

"Lord help me," Mary Stuart looked into her mirror. "Do you see lines in my forehead, Seton? Do I age with captivity?"

"Never, your Majesty." The woman expertly continued her brushing and kneading. "You are beautiful as ever."

The Queen of Scotland gave a little smile. "Aye, I believe men still covet me, Seton. The youngling with the flaming curls—I gave a fine performance before him, did

I not? He gave me his heart, Seton. He gave me his heart?"

Peevishly she shook her head free of the ministering fingers.

"Before long, Seton, I shall have the whole of this country kneeling at my feet, I promise you, and then the Queen of England and her precious Horsekeeper who beds with her, will dance to my tune. Only give me time, Seton, and it will all be mine!"

She gazed thoughtfully into her looking glass for a time.

"That youngling who carried away my letter to the Spanish Ambassador—do you know, I did not ask his name."

She yawned prettily, covering her mouth with elegant fingers.

"Ah, well," she said, "he was of no importance!"

FIVE

"No, MEG, you cannot go swithining! That is my last word!"

Anne knew it was not her last word, but she felt that after the events of the morning when she had surprised Kit and Meg in the wood by the edge of the meadow, some token of resistance was necessary.

"You are not to be trusted, Meg Weaver. You acted wrongly with Kit, this morning. Lord knows what might have happened to you."

"Kit would not have harmed me, Mother; besides, he is pledged to Amy Màrkenfield as I am pledged to Jeffrey."

Meg looked at the pattern her shoe toe traced in the farmyard dust.

"Pledges are promises, and promises were ever made to be broken, miss. Do you know that what you were doing could have got you with child? Do you realise that to lie so close to a man invites that which gets babies?"

"I know it, Mother. I have seen the animals . . ."

"Then why—?" Anne said, helplessly.

"I cannot tell you why. It just came about that way. I felt love for Kit, and it did not seem wrong." Earnestly,

Meg's eyes sought those of her mother. " I know now the feeling that loving brings, and I will take care not to let it happen again. And I am, Madam, sorry if I have hurt you."

Anne clucked impatiently. " You have not hurt me, Meg. You were nearer to hurting yourself." She pushed away a kitten that chased her broom. " I will let you go swithining if you agree to go with Jeffrey, and if you will promise not to speak to Kit, if he should be there. Will you give me your word, Meg?"

" That I will." Meg threw her arms round her mother's neck. " And I will be good, I promise you. I cannot be anything else," she added, wrinkling up her nose, " with old sobersides Jeffrey."

" You are wicked, miss. Jeffrey will make you a good husband."

" I know, Mother. Only give me time. It is all I ask. Give me time to get used to the idea, and I will wed Jeffrey on my eighteenth birthday. I promise you."

Anne placed an arm round Meg's shoulders. " You are a wilful girl, Meg Weaver. You are silly and spoiled, and your father and me love you dearly. Listen to what we have to say. We say it only for your good."

Meg is so beautiful, thought Anne. She has no idea how beautiful she is! And how very desirable. If only John had not sided with Meg when the betrothing was discussed. If only he had insisted that Meg and Jeffrey be married before the year-end. Two years was a long time to wait. There was nothing to stand in the way of the marriage. Indeed, with Jeffrey to share the farm work, John need not have worked so hard.

Anne raised her eyes skywards. Dear Lord, she thought, why did you not send me a dozen babies, that I might not centre all my love and emotions on Meg?

" Now get you gone, miss, and search the hedgerow for the brown hen's eggs. The day has been hot and long, and I still must prepare supper for Walter, and your father."

There was no harm in Meg, thought Anne, as she stirred the meat stew in the iron pot, but she was so wholly innocent that at times she could make a mother's blood run cold. Meg had never been allowed to go with the rest of the younglings of the village at the dawning of St. Swithin's Day and carry back flowers and boughs from the woods to adorn the church for the Swithintide service. Anne did not agree with it. It was pagan, she thought, to pray to the saint thus. Surely God in his wisdom knew better than any of his saints whether or not the good earth needed rain, be it for forty days, or four.

It was only an excuse, decided Anne, like the merry-making at Midsummer, for frolicking in the woods. It was sent, she was absolutely certain, to worry anxious mothers, and to provide opportunity for maids to lose their purity. At least, Jeffrey was more to be trusted than Kit. John could not thrash Kit for his misdeeds, for Kit was noble-born, and John was a yeoman.

Anne sighed, and threw dumplings into the stewpot.

Jeffrey was proud that the whole village knew of his betrothal to Meg, and that now they could openly walk out with fingers entwined or arms linked. He was so lucky to have been given Meg's pledge. She had always seemed so far above him, and she had always been Kit's play-fellow. Jeffrey had been both delighted and relieved when Kit's betrothal to Sir Thomas Markenfield's daughter had been made known.

Jeffrey had always secretly loved Meg, even when they had sat at the Dame's school together and laboriously chalked letters on their slates, but he had never dared hope Master Weaver would approach his father. His father, though, had been very pleased with the match, despite the fact that John Weaver was known to be well contented with the ways of the new church. He would be a good husband to Meg, Jeffrey silently vowed. He would work for her and protect her from all harm, once they were married.

" See, Meg, there is the sun." Jeffrey pointed to where the faint golden haze coloured the white mists of morning. " Now is the time to make your wish. Close your eyes, touch your heart, and wish hard; and I will do the same."

Meg did as she was bid. If only Kit were sitting beside her in the sweet cool dawn. If only it were Kit who held her hand and wished with her. Kit had not been there when the young people of the village set out for the woods. Perhaps he would join them later, for he had no sweetheart to take. Amy would not go swithining amongst village lads, and besides, her home was six miles away.

Meg wished fervently that it would suddenly be decreed that the daughter of a yeoman may marry the son of a nobleman, and she wished with all her heart that Sir Thomas Markenfield and his silly Amy could be transported to Ireland for failing to attend church each Sunday. There would be nothing at all then, to prevent her from marrying Kit.

"You make a long wish," laughed Jeffrey. "I hope with all my heart, sweet Meg, that it will come true for you."

"I hope so, too."

Meg felt guilty. She did not realise she had been wishing. No matter, it was done now. The wish was wished, and the die was cast.

"Did you make a wish, Jeffrey?" she asked.

She did not really care if he had wished or not, and it was nothing at all to her if it never came true, but she felt pity towards him.

Jeffrey was tall and straight, and his hair grew fair and thick. He loved Meg, and she could have come to love him, she was sure, if thoughts of Kit were not always with her. Meg wondered how it would feel to lie with him and get herself with child. Married people always got children, she knew that. She had always before thought it was part of being married. She had not thought it could be enjoyable to conceive a baby. But it had been enjoyable when she had lain beside Kit in the cool of the woodland, only half a day ago.

The feeling of love and desire she experienced had driven away all thoughts of shame or embarrassment. Her body had shivered when Kit had touched her, and she had wanted to press herself close to him and close her eyes and whisper words she would not have dared to say had she not been under the spell of his love. Words she knew could pass between no one but lovers. She wished her mother had not come between them. Perhaps if she had not, Meg thought, Kit's child would lie safely beneath her heart.

The sun touched the hedgerows, then rose higher and tipped the leaves of the tall woodland trees. Lazily a thrush chirped. Lifting its head, it sang an anthem to the morning. Reluctantly from grassy banks and sheltering bushes, the younglings of Aldbridge stretched their limbs and greeted the new day, their vigil over, their wishes made. Now they would collect blossoms and green boughs and musky-smelling ferns and take them to the church to please the good St. Swithin. There they would pray that he would hold back the rains for forty days so that the corn could be harvested.

Like Anne Weaver, Father Sedgwick did not hold with such foolish behaviour, but it pleased the simple people and one or two village maids secured husbands for themselves that without the help of the dawn watch and the shelter of the woodland might otherwise not have done so.

Leaving the road to walk his horse through the wood and on towards the village green, Kit came upon the bands of young lovers as, still blushing, they gathered their flowers. Meg was sitting on a grassy mound, her back resting on a young beech when Kit saw her. At her feet lay Jeffrey, his eyes full of calf love. Even after a ride to Castle Bolton and the journey back through the summer night, Kit could have done better than that, tired as he was.

They had not seen him, but if they had, their actions would have caused them no embarrassment. Stupid clod of a ploughman, thought Kit, as he gazed at Jeffrey, with distaste. What a waste of an opportunity! He had no right to be with Meg. Meg belonged to him, Kit Wakeman. Yesterday she had been all but his. She had been willing, and her soft body had stiffened and arched with delight at his touch.

She was so lovely. Her pale soft hair hung long over her face, swinging gently as she moved her head. How blue her eyes were. How soft and innocent the pure oval of her face. And Jeffrey, the peasant ploughman, would fondle Meg's tender body with his big rough hands, and it would be Jeffrey's child Meg would carry in her body.

Kit had not realised how much he had loved her. Now it was too late. He must marry Amy Markenfield, that he knew—plain solid Amy with her piggy eyes and her large child-bearing hips. Amy would be his wife and give him many children, but Meg would always be his love. Meg would be the one he would think of each night before he closed his eyes. Meg's lips would be the lips he kissed when Amy was in his arms.

Nothing on the face of the earth could change their separate destinies, but by Our Lady, Kit vowed, Meg would belong to him before she belonged to Jeffrey. Whatever happened, the first bite of the cherry would be Kit's. He could wait, and the waiting would make the triumph so much sweeter.

He pulled at his horse's head and gently walked the beast away from the sylvan setting.

SIX

THE RED winter sun that glowed like a beacon tinged the Christmas snow, and on the skyline the naked gibbet elm stood stark against a grey velvet sky. This was the fourth day of Christmas; the day upon which Sir Crispin Wakeman opened wide the great oak doors of the Manor to the whole of the village of Aldbridge. With eyes that sparkled and cheeks pinched red by the frosty air, Meg with her parents, and Goody Trewett her godmother, joined the stream of villagers on their way to the merrymaking.

Anne thought as she walked of the pleasure of visiting the manor house again. She had worked there as a young girl for Sir Crispin's parents, and later for Lady Hilda, and she knew and loved every corner of the old house. Now she felt the thrill of homecoming, for in some strange way, Anne looked upon the Manor as her other home.

There was nothing in Goody Trewitt's mind save thought of the food she would eat, for there was nothing in life that she liked better. Food was her child, her lover, and her comforter. All she asked of life was a full belly, and today she knew, life would be good to her.

John smiled his wide slow smile as Meg danced along ahead of them, begging them to hurry and forgetting that fat Goody could not and never did for that matter, walk at more than a snail's pace.

John looked at his daughter's happy face and felt a tightness in his throat at the beauty of her. Only yesterday, Goody had said that Meg was so fair she must surely have been a changeling left by the fairies. Dear Goody, who should have known better, since it was she who had helped Meg into the world and slapped the first cries of life into her.

As always, John counted his blessings. There had been a time during the long sweet summer when he had been afraid for his happiness, but the evil predicted by Walter Skelton had not touched his household. The summer past had been a good one, and lasted long into Michaelmas. The crops had been heavy and there had been no need to slaughter livestock for lack of winter keep. Milk and butter were still plentiful, and at New Year would come pig-killing time when the hard frosts of January boded well for bacon curing. Far up the dale John's twenty ewes, heavy with lambs were wintering in the care of a hill shepherd. Life, indeed, was good. And John Weaver was a happy man!

Soon I shall see Kit, quietly exulted Meg's heart. She had obeyed her mother and had not spoken to Kit since St. Swithin's Eve. She had seen him often and their eyes had said in passing what they must not say aloud. Now she was going to Kit's home for the Christmas festivities and her heart beat louder with every step that took her to him.

No matter what her mother commanded, she could not expect Meg to hide herself away from Kit today. At least she would be able to talk to him, perhaps even dance with him. Her fingertips tingled at the thought of touching his hand again, and her eyes shone because soon she knew they would be looking into Kit's eyes. Today Meg wore her best dress, and a cap of fine lace—a Christmas gift from her parents.

Yesterday Goody had called her beautiful. Maybe, thought Meg, it was because she loved Kit. Perhaps loving Kit had made her beautiful.

" Ho there!" Good Trewitt gave a shout. " Look at the Lord of Misrule. I'll wager that this year 'tis young Kit. See, Meg, what a fine figure he cuts!"

Laughing they hurried towards the youth dressed in jester's clothes, the bells on his cap tinkling with every movement of his head.

" The Lord of Misrule bids you welcome!"

There was no mistaking Kit, thought Meg, despite his clothes and the mask that covered his face.

With an exaggerated flourish, the Lord of Misrule kissed Goody's hand.

" I command that you eat and drink of the bounty of this house, for I am Lord of these festivities, and my every command must be obeyed."

With a sweep of his arm he ushered them into the warmth of the great hall where already half the villagers had gathered. The eyes behind the mask sought Meg's, and for a second in time held them in their gaze.

Meg looked at her toes and pulled her hood over her face, afraid that the blush that spread on her cheeks would betray her. She hoped Kit would take care and not alert her mother too much. Today Kit was King, for the word of the Lord of Misrule was law at such festivities, and whatever he should command or demand, all must obey, be it an order to a young gallant to kiss all the maids in the company, or sit with a fool's cap on his head and drink a gallon of old ale.

Meg prayed silently that Kit would tread carefully.

Anne looked about her. Each Christmas she loved this homecoming, for she knew to Lady Hilda she was a special favourite, and would be welcomed warmly in full view of the village. She dropped a curtsey before receiving a kiss of greeting from her old mistress.

Goody Trewitt made for the victuals table with an unusual swiftness whilst John walked over to the great fireplace where Christmas logs spat and burned and dried out the snow-damp breeches of ale drinkers. Meg looked around the massive room, softly lit by the glow of rush-lights and candles. The great black beams and rafters in the ceiling were higher even than those in the church. Surely they must almost touch the sky?

From behind his mask, Kit's eyes caressed Meg's slim body. The bodice of her dress clung to the curves of her firm young breasts and sprays of heartsease scattered themselves around the low-cut neckline. Had Meg sewn them there, thought Kit, to remind him of the hot day at haytime? And the words Meg had spoken! Soft, sad words about living again in a tiny wild pansy. Words that had made him fear for her immortal soul.

Kit's blood surged faster as he remembered that afternoon and the softness and nearness of Meg's body. On that

C

day, too, he had pledged his life to Mary Stuart, his Queen. In more ways than one, it had been a day he would not easily forget. He remembered still the hidden fire that smouldered within Meg—a fire still there for the lighting, if he could have his way.

And have it he would, Kit vowed, before the day was done.

Sir Crispin Wakeman walked towards John, his hand extended in greeting.

"Well met, John Weaver. Welcome to my house." He nudged John with his elbow and winked in the direction of Lady Hilda. "I'd wish the same to your good wife, Anne, could I but get a word in edgewise. See our women-folk; how they prattle!"

"Aye, their tongues clack like a weaver's shuttle," John laughed, taking Sir Crispin's hand in his. "Greetings, Sir Crispin. My family and I thank you for your hospitality."

Sir Crispin gave a low whistle. "Is that *your* little wench, John, who stands by the holly bough? I'faith, she has blossomed into a rare flower. It seems but yesterday she tumbled about the stable yard with Kit. See that you get her well betrothed, and quickly. I'd feel safer were she pledged, if she were mine!"

Together they walked to the table where already Goody Trewitt was licking her fingers and searching for the dish of marchpane. Sir Crispin handed a horn of ale to John, then poured one for himself.

"Do not worry, Sir Crispin. My little maid is already spoken for. She will marry Jeffrey, your ploughman, on her eighteenth birthday. We are very happy with the matching. Anne has a very warm corner in her heart for the young lad."

" He's a good boy," agreed Sir Crispin, " and I'll drink to that." He raised the horn he held in his hand. " To your pretty little Meg, and to her good betrothing. May they fill your house with fine children!"

As if to set the seal on their toast, there was a roll of drums from the gallery high above the hall, and the kitchen doors were flung open. To the sound of pipes and recorders and a great sigh of excitement, came scullions and kitchenmaids and spitboys, carrying high a boar's head. Stuffed with chopped pigmeat and herbs, blazed brown with bastings of honey and a red apple in its mouth, it seemed to Meg as she watched that the pig was enjoying itself hugely.

Behind the grinning pig's head came a spit-cooked swan on a great pewter dish, followed by a roasted peacock, stuck with a fan of feathers. And there was such a cheering and clapping that every burning minute of spit-turning and fat-spooning over the roasting fire, seemed now to have been worth while to those who had sweated in the kitchens.

Above the cheering the music signalled the start of the dancing and jigging, and the uproar echoed from the rafters and shook the garlands of ivy and holly and mistletoe. In a huddle beneath the minstrel's gallery, old women gossiped and young women danced and flirted, and barrel after barrel of Sir Crispin's ale was tapped whilst men laughed louder as whispered jokes became bawdier. Hands to her full stomach, mouth wide open, Goody Trewitt snored contentedly by the fire.

Gently, as she watched the surging crowd, a cool hand took Meg's.

"Will you dance the galliard, fair maid?" Kit's eyes laughed behind their mask. "You cannot refuse. The Lord of Misrule must be obeyed, and demands that you dance with him."

"Kit, love, I cannot. I have promised to dance only with Jeffrey." Meg held her hands to her burning cheeks. "We must not be seen together. My mother will start clucking like a hen, and I shall be bundled off home. Have a care."

"Meg, sweeting, I must talk to you." The Lord of Misrule's bantering tone was gone, and Kit's voice pleaded softly. "None will miss us in the noise of the dancing. I know a place where we can be alone for a while. Come with me, Meg."

He held out his hand, his voice softly pleading, and because Meg loved him, she did not protest.

"Quick now, make for the kitchens."

Holding Meg's hand, Kit kicked open the door with his foot. Safely through, they turned to each other and laughed. No one had seen them.

"This way."

They ran laughing across the stone floor, past the great table where the grease-covered spitboys made free with Sir Crispin's best ale and all the delicacies they had been able to filch.

"Ho there, young master!"

A groom held up his ale in salute, and the kitchenmaid on his knee giggled.

"What ho!" yelled Kit over his shoulder. "Good hunting, Gideon."

Then they were out of doors, and laughing with delight at their daring.

"There you are, Meg. None that mattered saw our flight, and those who did are too busy to bother."

Kit gathered Meg into his arms.

"You are trembling, sweetheart. It is cold here after the warmth of the house. Come with me. I know the snuggest place in all Christendom."

The cowshed was gloomy and only the breathing of the sleeping animals disturbed the quiet. The air was warm from the beasts' soft bodies, and the smell of newly-milked cows hung rich and earthy on the air. In a corner, a pile of hay with the breath of the hot summer meadows still upon it, reminded and suggested.

Kit snatched off his mask and threw down his jester's hat. With a soft tinkle of bells, it fell to the ground. He held out his arms to Meg and together, without speaking, they sank down beside it. The hay enfolded them with its warmth and she felt again the soft sinking sensation. She waited for the wave of triumph that would lift her up and relax her body into weightlessness.

"Kit?" Her body convulsed and arched itself and she pressed to him to stop her violent trembling. "Kit, love . . ."

He kissed the nape of her neck where a soft curl fell, then gently removed her lace cap. Her hair tumbled the hay and the roof above them became a tangle of green branches, and it was summer again.

Deliberately Kit held her at arm's length. He had waited so long, now he could savour the final seconds. He looked into her face and saw her eyes close in surrender, and her lips, slightly apart, searching for his own.

" Meg," he whispered. " Sweet little Meg of the Heartsease."

The wave came, and clasped together, they were borne high.

SEVEN

ANNE CAREFULLY returned the tiny garments to the chest and scattered them with lavender flowers, remembering sadly the last time she had fondled them. She had washed the little gowns, the delicate woollen shawl, and the bands of fine swaddling linen, and dried them in the summer sunshine, ready for the child that would be born about Lammastime. But her labour had started early and the child had not lived.

For the second time in three years she wept in Goody Trewitt's arms for a son that was stillborn and prayed to the Virgin Mother for comfort. That had been twelve years ago, and Anne had not conceived again. Now she accepted it as God's will, and that the beauty of the children she might have borne had been given in full to Meg, who was lovely beyond belief.

Anne wondered as she knelt there, how she could have been so blind. She should have guessed. How stupid Goody must now think her to be. She thought back to the wet cold day at the end of Lent when she had visited the old nurse, asking for a remedy.

" Meg sits and stares into the fire the whole day long,"

she had said. " She is interested in nothing; not even her food." Anne sat before the smoking fire in the midwife's cold little almshouse, her cloak hugged tightly around her. " There's something amiss with the maid, Goody. I'll be in your debt for a potion for her ailing stomach."

" If I had a potion to cure a Lenten stomach, I'd be rich as the Queen," Goody Trewitt snorted. " I'll swear by all that's holy the fish laws were the inspiration of the devil. Thank heaven our suffering will soon be over. God's Truth, I weary for the sight and taste of red meat."

" Salt fish never upset Meg's stomach before this," Anne spoke with more conviction than she felt. " There's a poison inside her that makes her puke and vomit whenever she eats. Come and see her, Goody. If anyone can help her it is yourself."

" Nay, Anne. There is nothing I can do. The maid has not taken kindly to her betrothal to Jeffrey. She sets you at defiance with her sulks."

Goody threw more logs on the fire and pulled her shawl around her shoulders.

" The day is too wet and cold for my old bones to stir outdoors. Depend upon it, there's nothing wrong with Meg that will not right itself once Lent is behind us, and we can be done with fasting and the eternal eating of salted fish."

At last Easter had come and the fish-days were behind them for another year. It had been good to eat the young lamb John killed in readiness for the feast day. That Easter they had prayed hard and loud in church for an end to the bad weather so that the farmers might plough their land and sow their corn. Anne had not remembered so bad a winter, and spring had come truculently with the April days tempestuous and cold. Meg's sickness had not vanished as Goody predicted, and once again Anne had sought help.

" Let old Nurse see for herself this poor ailing belly," Goody had said only that morning as she hobbled into the warmth of Anne's kitchen, her words spoken lightly as if to humour a doting mother. " I'll grant you the maid looks pinched about the face, good Anne, but it's the foul weather at the root of it all."

The teasing smile left Goody's face.

" Lord's sake, mistress, where are your eyes? There's one remedy alone for this. Get the maid wed, and soon! "

" In God's good time." Anne's mind rejected the offered advice. " Her father does not wish her marriage until her eighteenth birthday."

" Then you'll have a bastard for a grandchild long before that day comes! "

How could one so sensible suddenly turn so stupid, wondered Goody.

" *Meg is with child*! " She spoke the words harshly that they might penetrate the barrier of disbelief Anne had thrown around herself.

Slowly Goody walked to the door. " You'll need me in the late summer, if my eyes and reasoning have not deserted me. There's nothing I can do till then. It's the words of a priest you need now."

Meg began to cry quietly and her sobs drove home the truth of Goody's words. Anne covered her face with her hands and sank to her knees.

" Mother of God, help me! " she pleaded.

c*

"Your prayers fly in the wrong direction. Pray to St. Anthony that he might find for you the one who got her that way!" Goody said from the doorway.

She looked at Meg's small face and Anne's kneeling figure that shook with sobbing.

"Good friend," she said, "do not fret. Meg is not the only maid in Aldbridge who got herself a love child at Christmas. It will all come out in the washing."

Anne closed the lid of the chest and slowly rose to her feet, Goody's prophecy still sounding in her ears. *It will all come out in the washing*. And what stinking washing! In her wisdom Goody had left Anne alone, muttering damnation to all men as she waddled away. In the little room in the farmhouse eaves, Meg lay on her bed, her quiet sobbing tearing at Anne's heart. With shame Anne remembered her reaction to Goody's pronouncement.

"Slut!" she had yelled. "Sly little strumpet! You are no longer my daughter. Go to him that dirtied you, for the sight of you sickens me!"

She had not meant to strike out so violently. Meg lay where she had fallen, crouching in the shelter of the table.

"Madam, for pity's sake, forgive me, I beg you."

But there had been no pity in Anne's heart.

Now, suddenly, Anne wanted John by her side. She needed his strength and the feel of his arms protecting her from the nightmare. John would know what was best to be done. By now he should have sold the cloth he had taken to Ripon, and be on his way home.

John had not idled during the winter when the land had been too sad and wet to work on. He had spent those days in the weaving loft. If the land would not give them a living in the coming year, then John's loom would.

Anne's heart ached at the goodness in him as she knelt by the fire, hugging her grief around her. Meg and John were her whole life. No one else existed. Nothing else had mattered. Anne should have known such happiness would have to be paid for, and now reckoning day had come. She closed her eyes and willed John home.

" What is to be done?" Anne asked yet again. " Meg is ruined. None will take her now."

" Anne love," John spoke quietly, " the end of the world has not yet come. Goody may be wrong."

" Then why did Meg not deny it?" Bitterly Anne flung out the words. " And have you ever known Mistress Trewitt to be wrong?"

John shook his head. " No, but we do not know the one who fathered the bairn. Perhaps he will marry Meg. Did she tell you his name?"

" She did not, for I did not ask her." Anne did not lift her eyes from her tightly clasped hands. " I know nothing, but I'll swear it is none of Jeffrey's doing. It's a late summer baby, so it was gotten at Christmas. It could be any of half a score young gallants!"

" No, Anne!" John protested at his wife's directness. " If the babe was of Christmas getting then I fear for Meg. She had eyes for no one save Kit, and Kit cannot marry her."

" So it is as I said," Anne retorted. " None will have her now, and she could not marry out of her station, even if Kit were willing to have her in wedlock."

" Jeffrey?" hazarded John.

" No. His father would never agree to the marriage now.

He would not let Jeffrey take Meg with another's child.
Meg must be made to confess her wrong-doing, and if it is
Kit Wakeman's child, he must pay for his bastard."

Anne took her cloak from the door peg.

" Speak to her, John, for i'faith, I cannot. Maybe a walk
will cool my temper."

Anne looked up to the open door at the head of the
staircase. Meg had awakened and her desolate sobbing
could once more be heard.

" She cries afresh, and it tears at my heart to hear it."
Anne's voice trembled on the verge of tears. " God's
pity, could she could cry the thing out of her womb!"

The door slammed and all was quiet, save for the
crackling of burning logs and the cries that seemed to John
to be born of the very dregs of despair. First he would
talk to Meg, and then he would go to the Manor to see
Sir Crispin. John squared his shoulders. Sir Crispin, he
knew, would not fail him . . .

" I did not skulk like a thief in the night." John denied
his wife's accusation much later. " The front of the Manor
was shuttered and I walked to the back of the house. I
tell you, Anne, I saw them. They sat round the table in
the great kitchen."

" The *kitchen*?"

" Where else would they sit when the builders and
stonemasons have taken possession of the house: I tell
you they sat in the kitchen—almost a dozen men."

" But who were these men?"

" Some of them I did not know, but Sir Thomas
Markenfield was there, and Sir Richard Norton and two
of his sons,"

" And I suppose they shouted their business out loud so that John Weaver might hear it?" Anne would not be convinced.

" No, Anne. You know of the pastry kitchen that opens off the great kitchen—the one with the iron bars for a window?"

" I should do," Anne Weaver pulled down the corners of her mouth, " for I spent many a cold hour in it."

" That is how I heard what they said, Anne. The door between the kitchens was left ajar, though they did not know it. Their voices came plain to me as I stood by the grille."

" Do you remember," Anne smiled fondly, " that you often kissed me through that grille?"

" I remember, love. If only those days were with us again. If only I were that young apprentice who crept in the dark for a kiss."

" John, love." Anne took her husband's hand in hers. " You could be mistaken. You were beside yourself when you went to the Manor. Did you perhaps not hear aright?"

John Weaver stared into the fire.

" I knew my journey would come to nothing. I knew evil would happen this night. The omen in the churchyard foretold it. It was the fox's head!"

Anne sat motionless. Despite her Catholic soul, she believed in omens.

" I saw Barnabas there in the moonlight, nailing a fox's head to the church door. The animal was not long dead and its blood traced out the carving on the door and fell on to the steps of the church. It looked evil."

"No, husband," soothed Anne, "the hunchback needs the money he earns from his fox catching. How else could he claim his bounty if he did not nail the heads to the door of the church? Perhaps it looked evil because you stood in the graveyard."

"I tell you, Anne, blood will run in Yorkshire 'ere long. The year started badly, and it will end badly!"

"Tell me what you heard, John. I cannot rightly grasp the meaning of it all."

"They drank a toast to the Queen. In Sir Crispin's kitchen they raised their goblets and toasted her in wine."

"And do you not above all people think that is good?"

"No, Anne, I do not, for the toast was in a language that was foreign to me. I knew the name, though—it was Marie. They drank to Scottish Mary—not our own Elizabeth—and well they might, for I'll swear that all present were of the Catholic faith."

"And would it be such a bad thing," Anne challenged, "if we were to have a Catholic Queen on England's throne again?"

"Yes, Anne, it would, for it would take civil war in the land to put Mary Stuart on Elizabeth's throne. I have heard talk passed down by the old ones about civil war. We can live well without it. These last ten years have been peaceful. There have been no heretics burned and men may follow the Catholic faith so long as they do it quietly. Can they not be content with that?"

John threw logs on the fire.

"Did you make your peace with Meg whilst I was gone?"

" Yes, though I am still sorely troubled. What is to be done?"

John took Anne's hands and pulled her to her feet.

" To bed with you, wife, and leave the troubling to me. I shall do what is right for us all. You must promise you will say nothing to a living soul of what I have heard and seen this night—not even to Goody! "

John pinched out the candle flame. He could think better by firelight. He had intended to tax Sir Crispin with young Kit's behaviour, for Meg had admitted to John, between her sobs, that the child she carried could only belong to Kit. John had not bargained for what he had learned that night as he stood by the open grille of the pastry kitchen.

Was it really less than a year ago that Walter Skelton had warned of a foreboding of evil? He remembered the Tyneside carter and his sea-coal. John knew now that the sea-coal had been a cover for what had been hidden underneath, and that bows and arrows and pikes and armour were secreted away in great quantities in the houses of Catholic nobles.

Those men had talked of the help that would come for their cause from Spain. They had spoken of de Spes, the Spanish ambassador to Elizabeth's court and the Duke of Alva, and a letter Mary Stuart had sent from Tutbury. Thank God, thought John, that at least the Scottish Queen had been moved from Castle Bolton.

Sir Richard Norton had told of the letter. It had been smuggled from the Midlands by a Stuart loyalist and taken to de Spes. *Tell your master,* it had said, *that if he will help me, I shall be Queen of England in three months, and Mass shall be said over all the Kingdom.*

And they had answered " Deo Volente "—*God willing.*
John knew its meaning from the Latin chantings of the
old days. Was God willing to spill blood so that the stench
of burning Protestant flesh might once again taint the air
of Smithfields? What crimes were committed in God's
name?

Of one thing John was certain. He would go no more
to the Manor and ask help of Sir Crispin. Sir Crispin was
taken up with other matters, for surely he improved the
Manor in anticipation of rewards to come? Nor would
John accept help from one who sought to overthrow the
Queen.

Perhaps he could send Meg to York, to Anne's cousin?
Could he and Anne, when the baby was born, claim it was
their own? It had been known for women of Anne's age
to bear a living child. Would this be wrong? Would
Goody aid their deception? It could hurt no one and may
yet save Meg's marriage to Jeffrey. But Jeffrey might grow
suspicious.

There was still a year to run before he and Meg were
pledged to wed. A lot could happen in a twelvemonth.
Peter, Jeffrey's father, was a Catholic, and slaved to pay
the shilling fines for all his family so that they might not
offend their consciences by worshipping in the English
church. It was likely that Jeffrey would take up arms for
Mary Stuart. Would he live to tell of it if he did?

The light touch of Meg's fingers caused him to turn.
She stood wraith-like, her face white as her night-
shift.

" Sir? " Her eyes pleaded for comfort. John held out

his arms and she ran into them. Gently he stroked her hair. " There now, little one, it will be all right."

The blue eyes that looked up into John's filled with tears.

" Father, I do love you so. Forgive me?"

Words did not come easily to John in times of emotion. He kissed the top of her head and held her close. Of one thing suddenly, he was certain. The whole of England could run with blood if only Meg could be spared one moment of torment.

By God's Death, John vowed silently, *if harm comes to one soft lock of her hair, then he who has caused it shall suffer!*

EIGHT

"IT IS not right," Anne said as she laid John's breakfast on the table, "that Jeffrey should be so deceived. He must be told. He cannot be held now to his marriage pledge."

John stared at the plate before him, his appetite gone.

"It may be," he said, "that Jeffrey might still want to marry Meg, despite the child."

"Jeffrey might want to, if the choosing were left to him. But would his father allow it? Jeffrey would be the laughing-stock of the village when folks realised he'd been cuckolded. There is nothing for it. He must be told; or Meg must tell him she does not wish to marry him."

"And what then will happen to Meg?" John's practical common sense was not concerned with rights or wrongs. "She cannot stay here after the babe is born, right under Kit's nose. It will not be long now before Kit is wed and brings his bride home to Aldbridge. How will Meg fare when his lady-wife comes face to face with Kit's bastard?"

"Not very well, I should imagine," Anne was forced to admit. "I have heard it said that Mistress Amy has a waspish temper."

Anne was wavering and John was quick to press home his advantage.

"Do you want to send Meg to York to relatives she hardly knows? Do you want our first grandchild to be born amongst near-strangers? It is not right, Anne."

"It is not right, John. I know it now. It must be as you say. We must say the babe is our own. Only Goody knows Meg's secret. Perhaps God in His wisdom prevented you from seeing Sir Crispin, for had you told him we could not have played out the deceit." She blushed, and gave a little laugh. "Does it please you, John Weaver, that you are to be a father again?"

Relieved beyond measure, John smiled into Anne's eyes.

"It pleases me, my love. What I do not like are the lies we have to tell. And Goody must agree to the deception or it will be no good. But I am well pleased. We must hope and pray it can be done."

True friend that she was, Goody Trewitt readily consented to their plan.

"Does it matter who fathers a babe or who mothers it? It is one of God's creatures. That is all that matters," she said bluntly.

"I would not have asked it, but it can do no wrong, and it can bring about a lot of good." John laid his arm around her shoulders. "You are a good friend, Mistress Nurse."

Goody took John's hand. "And you are all the family I have now. You are dearer to me than any of my own ever were. If any of you is scratched, then Goody Trewitt will bleed for you. What do a few little lies matter? Why, they are so ordinary that I'll wager Father Sedgwick will absolve the lot of them in exchange for a pot of my salve for his back-ache."

Anne and John had reckoned without Meg. At first she wept when they told of their plan, and then she pleaded to be allowed to see Kit.

" Kit loves me. Our babe is a true love-child," she sobbed. " We will go to York together to the Catholic priest. Kit will marry me, I know it. Only let me tell him, I beg of you."

" Meg, little bird," John took Meg's hands in his and forced her to meet his eyes. " It can do no good. Kit will not have you. He cannot wed you. He is pledged to one whose station in life is equal to his own."

Meg stared rebelliously ahead of her, chin tilted, her lips held tight to stop their trembling.

" I must see Kit," she insisted. " I *will* see him."

" Then come to where I am standing. Come here, miss, and you can see your lover for the asking!"

Roughly Anne took Meg's shoulders and pushed her towards the window.

" See them? There is your Kit, and with him Miss Amy. See what a fine couple they make as they ride past. No doubt he is showing her the lands that will one day be his, lands that one day he will pass on to the son *she* gives him. Your little child will never own Aldbridge, Meg. See how well the Markenfield wench sits her horse, Meg. She surveys the village as if she were already lady of the manor house."

Anne shook with rage, for the sight of Kit's betrothed, laughing and carefree and contrasting so sadly with Meg's unhappiness, was hard for her to stomach.

"Do you see your lover, Meg? A man only courts a maid until he catches her. You should have said no to him a little longer. Now he has had you, you are nothing to him. I'll warrant Amy will not sell herself so cheap!"

The fresh flood of tears Anne expected of Meg did not come. The sight of Kit and Amy riding together through the village brought home to Meg the utter futility of the situation.

"Tell me what I am to do, madam, and I will obey you," she added quietly.

The capitulation was too easy. Meg's acceptance of the demands of her parents did not ring true. Anne was uneasy, and caught off her guard.

"Do nothing yet awhile. Just hold your tongue and give me time to think. Above all, steer clear of Kit Wakeman, or I'll whip you round the house!"

Meg turned away from the window and without a backward glance walked up the staircase to her bedroom.

Anne looked about her in bewilderment.

"Her face was set like a mask." She turned to her husband, apprehensive and suddenly afraid. "She was too calm, John. She will do something foolish and sinful, I know it!" Suddenly her voice rose to near-hysteria. "Damn you, Kit Wakeman. May your vile seducing body rot in hell. May the carrions pick out your eyes and the devil take your heart for a football!"

Goody held up her hand as John hastened to comfort Anne.

"Leave her," she cautioned. "Nothing you can say will help. Tears are her best medicine."

Quietly, John and Goody left the room.

" It would be better," said Goody as she walked towards the garden gate with John, " if Meg were to tell Jeffrey herself that she cannot marry him yet awhile, and she must be quick about it, for soon her condition will show and he will guess the real truth. Meg will find the best words to use. The young have a bond between them. The boy will understand better if it comes from Meg."

Goody pulled the hood of her cloak over her head, for the late April night was cold and wet.

" It will do her good to sort out her own troubles. You and Anne have spoiled and sheltered her for too long. Let her grow up a little and start living her own life. Let her forage for herself. It is better that way."

Grumbling about the damp in general, and men in particular, Goody made for her little cottage by St. Olave's churchyard.

" I knew when I awoke this morning it would be a good day." Shyly, Jeffrey reached for Meg's hand. " The birds were singing their little hearts out, and the sun shone early. I think that winter has gone at last. Given a good drying wind, I will be able to put the plough on to the land tomorrow."

He looked at Meg's face and blushed.

" I am sorry, Meg. I have not seen you for many days, and I can only talk about the land. Maybe, though I did not know it, the good feeling I knew this morning was because the birds were trying to tell me I would see you."

Anxiously he looked at Meg, hoping that his stumbling efforts at love-talk had made their mark.

" I am not a good wooer, am I, Meg? I am not good

with words, but I love you dearly. Will you believe me?"

"I believe you, Jeffrey. Truly I believe you." The words were scarcely above a whisper. "You are good and kind, and that is better by far than a glib tongue."

Awkwardly, the boy blushed with pleasure.

"I have news for you, Meg. My mother's brother who farms his own land at Stavely has broken his leg. The bone-setter says he must not walk on it for several months, and so my uncle has sent for me. I am to work his land until he recovers. He will pay me well, Meg, and Sir Crispin has agreed I can go if I first plough his fields."

Anxiously he searched Meg's face for some kind of answering emotion, some small token, perhaps that she would miss him.

"I will try to see you sometimes, even though it is eight miles from Stavely," he added.

"I am glad for you, Jeffrey, that your uncle thinks so highly of you."

"Will you miss me, Meg?"

He was eager for a word of praise from her; eager for some small crumb of comfort. Yet try as he may, Jeffrey could not break the barrier Meg seemed to have thrown up between them.

"I will miss you, Jeffrey."

Meg's heart gave a little bound of hope. Perhaps now she need not tell Jeffrey she would not marry him. Perhaps, if he were not able to find the time to travel from Stavely to Aldbridge, it would be easier for her to keep her secret.

" I do not want to go, Meg, you should know that, but
I have a mind for my bride to have a gold wedding
ring!"

" A *gold* ring, Jeffrey?"

" Aye, Meg. My mother was not wed with a ring, and it
was many years before she had one, and then only of
common gold. I want you to have a fine ring of pure gold
on your wedding day. If I work hard on my uncle's farm,
I will be able to buy one for you, and a fine wedding gown
into the bargain."

" Oh, Jeffrey!"

Meg covered her face with her hands and wept. He was
so good. So eager to please her. So shy, and so very
gentle.

Jeffrey reminded Meg of her own father, and the loving
way he always looked at her mother. She could, she knew,
have come to love Jeffrey. Never with the same abandoned
passion she felt for Kit. That kind of love would never
come again. Kit had been her first love and she would
always remember him, no matter what happened. However well Amy might sit a horse, or scream at the servants
at the Manor, however many fine sons she might give to
Kit, nothing would wipe from Meg's heart the sweet
memory of the feeling of wonderment they had known
together.

Meg would always know the day—almost the very hour
she had conceived their child. What better day than
Childermas to make a new life?

" Sweetheart." Diffidently, Jeffrey took her in his arms.
" Don't cry. I will come and see you every week, I promise.
Even if I walk through the night, I will come. I am

glad you weep for me, though I wish you would not do it."

"No, Jeffrey, it is not that." Meg shook her head. She must tell him now. He was too good to hurt. "I cry because I am not sure of my feelings for you. I want to be right in what I do, and at this moment I am confused. That is why I asked you to meet me, Jeffrey. I wanted to tell you."

"You mean you will not marry me?" He whispered the words through lips help tight with disbelief. "What has happened to you, Meg? Who has come between us?"

"No one has come between us," Meg lied. *Only my beloved Kit and the child I carry*, whispered her heart! *Only they have come between us, Jeffrey.* "It is just that I am not ready for marriage yet. I know we are not to marry for another year, but maybe if you go to Stavely you will meet another girl who will make a better wife for you, than I. If you do, Jeffrey, I will not hold you to our pledge."

Steadfastly he looked into Meg's eyes.

"There will never be another but you, I swear it. I have known you did not love me, but those who know better than I, tell me that love *will* follow. I would not have asked anything of you, Meg, until you were ready to give it to me. Will you not think again about what you have said?"

"I will think about it, Jeffrey. Will you promise me one thing?" She hated herself for what she was doing. She was lying and cheating. She deserved to suffer, she knew it. "Go to your uncle's house at Stavely. It will be well that you do. Do not try to see me in that time, and my feelings for you will be better known to me when you return. I am confused and unsure; and there are other reasons."

"Tell them to me, Meg," Jeffrey said as he stared ahead, his gentle face contorted with misery.

"My mother is with child. It is serious at her age to bear a child, and she must rest, Goody says, and not lift heavy weights as though she were a man. If she is careful, my mother and the babe should do well, but I must care for her and do more work about the house."

Meg licked her dry lips. It would not have surprised her if her tongue had turned to paper and dropped out of her mouth with all the lies it was telling. She had not thought that the love between herself and Kit could have caused so much heartache. But for all the unhappiness, Meg could still not deny one precious minute of the time she had spent in Kit's arms, not even with Jeffrey's arms folded round her in comfort.

"Dear little Meg. How like you to think first of your mother. I understand your feelings, and I love you all the more for them. It is as well that I am going to Stavely. I will not try to see you during the time I am away. Perhaps in the late summer when I return you will know your true feelings. It is said that absence makes the heart grow tender."

For a moment Meg wanted to pour out her heart to the kind youth who stood beside her. She wanted above all to tell him the whole truth and to stop the web of deceit they had all begun to spin, and must now spin faster to cover every lie. But there was not only her own conscience to consider. There was her mother and her father and the babe to think about.

There was Kit, as well. He must never know about their child. It would be wrong of her, Meg decided, to hurt so many people. And if the tangle of lies around them were not discovered and the babe when it was born was accepted as her mother's, then Meg silently vowed, she would marry Jeffrey, and make up to him as best she could for the unhappiness she was causing him.

"I hope it will do that, Jeffrey. I will pray that it will, and I will think of you whilst you are away. You are my very dear friend."

She placed her finger tips on his cheek, then stood on tiptoe and gently kissed his lips.

"God go with you, dear Jeffrey," she whispered through her tears.

NINE

" 'Tɪs ᴡᴇʟʟ that Meg carries the babe in her back," Goody Trewitt said, " and not out in front of her for all the world to see. It will be a boy, for sure."

" I don't care whether it's a boy or a girl. I only know I am heartily sick of this deception," Anne said angrily.

There was gleaning to be done in the cornfield and it was not thought fitting that a pregnant woman of Anne's age should labour in the fields. All the burden of the harvest must fall on John's already tired shoulders, for Meg could not show herself.

" God, I hate these lies. I am sick of wearing my winter cloak to hide a babe I do not carry. I am tired of pretending an illness that keeps Meg housebound to tend me! Will this deception never end?"

" Aye, Anne, it will. Meg is near her time. The babe will be born soon—perhaps even on your birthday tomorrow."

Anne sighed and stirred the broth that simmered over the fire.

" A babe in my thirty-seventh year? Have you ever

known it, Goody? Have you ever before delivered a woman so old?"

"That I have, Anne Weaver, that I have!"

Anne handed a bowl of broth to the old midwife.

"I fear we will pay dearly for these lies. Our sins must surely find us out. I watch Meg like a hawk for fear she will show herself without a loose apron to hide her body. Sometimes I feel no good will come of it."

"It is too late to recant now, for the whole village believes you are with child. Bear with Meg a few days more. She suffers inwardly. And think not that you will have to answer for your sins. Is it wrong to protect a maid from shame, or a babe from bastardy? I'll warrant Father Sedgwick has listened to worse sins in his time."

Anne pursed her lips and indicated the door with a movement of her head.

"Meg comes. Hush!"

Meg took off her cloak and lifted her damp hair from the nape of her neck.

"Lord, 'tis hot! Father says there will be a storm before sundown."

"You have been to the field in daylight? Foolish maid! Who saw you?"

"None saw me, madam, of that I am sure." Meg shook her head at the broth her mother offered. "I thank you, but I am not hungry."

She placed her hands in the small of her back and paced the kitchen floor.

"Lord, I grow sick of walking out at night so none may see me."

"Then you should have waited, miss, until wedlock

made your condition respectable," snapped Anne. " Do you think we enjoy this play-acting? And Goody must share our deceit, too. Would I had a sovereign for every lie she has put about to shield you!"

" 'Tis as John says," clucked Goody. " A storm brews. It makes us all tetchy. Go to your bedroom, Meg love, and sit by the window. You will be cooler there."

From the tiny window Meg watched the clear summer sky take on a yellow light. Birds were silent and in the field, John sweated to gather in the last of the wheat before the deluge came. Every ear of corn was precious. The spring sowings had been late, and the summer a wet one. There was little hay, and the corn harvest was equally poor. Already merchants were buying what grain could be spared and the prices they offered made it impossible for the poor to compete with them. Many a man with an empty belly and whimpering children would pay his debt to hunger with a severed right hand before another harvest was gathered. There would be famine in the land, John knew, even before the winter set in.

The swarm of beggars that had been whipped out of York already knew the bite of hunger. Flinging oaths at the militia men who saw them on their way, they made for open country, where pickings would be better and the law less rigorous. Devil take any who stood in the way of the angry mob as it rampaged through field and orchard, stealing anything that still grew before it, and streamed on to yet another village.

Meg from her seat at the window, heard the cry of the child who ran from Gibbet Hill shouting the alarm.

" The beggars are coming. The beggars are coming! Let loose your dogs!"

Men who heard the call ran to their homes from the fields and women scooped up their children and their tethered hens and slammed and bolted their doors.

The mob was hungry. Their mood was ugly. They demanded food of Father Sedgwick. But the priest yelled at them from his bedchamber window to be gone, so they spat on his door and teemed through the graveyard, and on towards the Green.

Meg knew they were heading for the Manor; knew too, that Sir Crispin was away in Ripon. A desperate longing came over her. She wanted to see Kit again and tell him about their child. Since Easter she had been almost a prisoner, going out only when darkness shielded her; seeing no one. She was still ashamed of the way she had treated Jeffrey. He had believed every lie she had told him, and had been as good as his word. He had accepted all she had asked of him with never a protest, and had not tried to see her.

Jeffrey was good—like her father. Married to Jeffrey she would have been loved and cosseted as her mother was. She liked Jeffrey; perhaps in time she would love him, but she belonged, and would always belong in her heart to Kit. Now she carried Kit's child, and Kit did not know. Nor could Meg tell him because her parents, in their goodness, played out a lie like actors on a stage, to protect the babe from shame.

From her window Meg had often seen Kit and longed to run to him. Now some strange stirring within her demanded that she did. She would pull her cloak around

her—she would not tell him about the child, merely warn
him of the approaching mob. Kit must call back the work-
men from the fields. And she must tell him of what her
father knew of the meeting in the Manor kitchen. She
must warn him to have a care, that their plans were known
to her father.

Somehow, Meg thought wildly, she must get to Kit
without being seen. The stone wall would protect her
until she reached the wood. Once she was in the wood,
it would be easy.

" Lord help us, child, what are you about?" called
Goody as Meg snatched her cloak from the door-peg.
" The storm approaches. You will be drenched. Mistress
Anne, the maid has taken leave of her senses! Bring her
back, I beg of you!"

But Meg had reached the shelter of the wood almost
before they realised she was gone. Slowly and deliberately
the deluge began, and the thunder grumbled closer.

Jeffrey heard the same thunder, and was glad. A storm
would clear the air, for the hot sultry weather made
walking hard. He wondered if Meg's father had harvested
his wheat and rye, and if Sir Crispin's men were still
working in the fields. He thought with pleasure of the
three sovereigns his uncle had given him when the harvest
was safely in.

" You have worked well, lad," his uncle had said. " I
shall feel the happier that my land will come to you when
I die."

In the pack on his back was a length of blue silk
bought only that morning in the market place at Ripon.
He hoped with all his heart that Meg would wear it on

their wedding day. Jeffrey quickened his step. The sooner he were home, the sooner he would see Meg.

A jagged flash of lightning forked earthwards and thunder crashed and echoed before it rumbled away to the hills.

The rain beat into Meg's face as she left the shelter of the wood. Ahead of her she could see the Green and the manor house. She was too late, she knew. Try as she might, Meg could not outrun the yelling beggars. They ran abreast of her then closed in around her, carrying her with them as they surged on. She was helpless against the hungry mob, each man fighting and jostling so that he might get to the Manor gates before they were closed.

" Kit!" Meg called, but her voice was carried away on a clap of thunder.

" Give us food!" yelled the mob, as the gates crashed together. " We ask but a crust for our children! The saints will bless you if you give us food!"

Atop the thick stone wall stood Sir Crispin's men, pitchforks and lances at the ready.

" Get you all gone from this place," shouted Kit, " or I'll hang every last man of you!"

" Food!" demanded the mob. " Give us food!"

They pressed forward, those nearest the gates groping with their hands through the bars to find the latch. Their evil-smelling bodies pressed close to Meg. The stench made her want to vomit. They smelled like filthy animals. They looked like animals, and like animals they were vicious when hungry.

" Kit, I must speak to you!" She cried out in fear as

D

she was jostled and bruised by the beggars. "Let me through, I must speak with Kit."

"Hold there!" Hands grabbed at Meg's shoulders. "Hold your tongues!" The angry demanding became a confused babble. "Silence, I say." There was a hushing sound, then all was quiet.

"We have here," called the man whose filthy hands grasped Meg's shoulders, "a maid who would speak with the young master yonder. Let her through, that she may plead our case with the fine young coxcomb. Let the maid through, I say!"

The stinking crowd parted, and Meg was thrust forward until she came face to face with Kit. From either side of the gates they faced each other.

"Kit, sweetheart, I must tell you." Tears brimmed from her eyes and mingled with the rain that ran down her cheeks. "They wouldn't let me see you, and they wouldn't let me tell you. Help me, Kit. Don't turn me away."

"She asks help, young master. We all ask help. Your barns are full of grain, and you have cattle in your fields. Spare us a little of your plenty, young sir, and spare a little of your pity for this maid."

"I'll spare you nothing," Kit brandished his sword, brave with a dozen of his father's men at his back, "and I have nothing to say to the maid!"

Why did Meg torment him at such a time? Had he not enough trouble without a weeping girl to contend with?

"Go home, Meg Weaver. This is no place for you. Get you gone before you come to harm."

"No, Kit, no!" Meg clung to the gates, afraid lest

the jostling elbows and flailing fists should knock her to the ground. " I came to warn you; to tell you to be careful. My father knows of the meetings at your house. I heard him speak of it to my mother. He knows what you plan to do. I come to tell you of this. Take care, Kit, for he knows your secret! "

" Ho! The young coxcomb has a secret and one I'll warrant he'll pay to preserve! " Grasping the hair that lay wet on Meg's cheeks he forced her to face the mob. " Now, sweet maid, will you tell us the young master's secret, or does he give us bread and meat for its safekeeping? What shall it be, young sir? "

The bailiff who stood beside Kit narrowed his eyes.

" What does she mean, Master Kit? Do you betray the cause? God's blood, lad, deny it and quick, or this rabble will be shouting it in the streets of London before you have time to wink an eye! "

" Damn you for the louts you are! " Kit turned to the yelling mob. " I give you no bread and I give you no meat, for there is no secret to tell. Would you take the word of a witch before the word of a gentleman? She lies, I tell you. She lies! "

A murmur of surprise whispered through the crowd.

" She is not a witch! " called a voice from the edge of the crowd. " Meg Weaver is no witch! " Jeffrey called, desperately pushing and struggling to reach Meg.

" And I say she is a witch! " flung back the bailiff, snatching at the reprieve. " Tell them, young master. Tell them of her spells. "

The shock of Meg's words had stunned Kit. Now, prompted by his father's servants, he warmed to his lies.

" That wench is a witch, I tell you. She believes that we can take another form! Who but a witch would say that? She says that when our immortal souls leave our bodies they come again to this earth as a beast of the fields, or a flower that grows! Are these not the rantings of a witch?"

The crowd drew back from the gates. Several of the ragged women crossed themselves. The man who had pushed Meg forward wiped his hands down his rags as though to wipe away the touch of one so tainted.

" Kit! Oh, Kit!" sobbed Meg.

Her ears were deceiving her. She had not heard aright. This was not Kit who shouted such madness to the mob. This was not the lover who had kissed her eyelids and made her flesh tingle with longing at the touch of his hands. This could not be the beloved whose strong young body had lain beside her own and given her his child.

" Kit, love," her words were a scream of anguish. She turned to gaze at the hostile faces about her. " He lies," she sobbed. " He lies!"

" No, good people, I do not lie. Why do you think your bellies meet your backbones? Is it not the doing of witches such as this?" He pointed a finger at Meg. " It is they who make our crops fail? They cast their spells, and our cattle die. Offend one of her ilk and she will whistle up the east wind to wither the fruit on the trees! She is a witch, I tell you. *A witch!*"

" Aye!" roared the bailiff. The mob quiet now, almost afraid. " The young master speaks the truth. Be gone from here, lest she casts her evil eye on you. Be gone!"

But the beggars stood their ground. Their bellies ached

with hunger and they wanted food. The doors and windows of the village were shuttered against them for the villagers had no food to give. And there was no food because the crops had failed, and the crops had failed because the east winds had withered the tender young shoots of spring. Witches whistled up the east wind. Witches were evil!

" Stone the witch!" went up the cry. If they wouldn't have food then they would have sport. " Stone the witch!"

A cobble hurtled through the air and crashed against the Manor gate above Meg's head.

" Help me," she. pleaded. " Help me, Kit."

" Witch! Witch! Stone the witch!" mocked the tattered children and jumped for joy at the spectacle.

" Help me, Kit!"

Meg shielded her head with her arms, and cobblestones hurtled through the air whilst the crowd jeered and laughed.

" Kit, they will kill me!"

But Kit stood silent behind the bars of the great oak gates.

The cobble hit Meg's head with vicious force. A pain shot between her eyes and a black cloud enveloped her head. She sank to the ground without a sound and lay there still.

" God, Master Kit, they've killed her!" a servant gasped, and hurriedly crossed himself.

Passion gone, hunger forgotten, the mob inched forward. One by one, Sir Crispin's retainers jumped from the wall and ran, wanting nothing to do with the witch hunt. From the edge of the crowd a youth pressed forward, flinging aside those who stood in his way.

"God damn you all!" Jeffrey turned to face the mob, his face white with anger. "Did you not hear my warning? This maid is no witch!" He pointed to the trickle of blood that ran from the wound at Meg's temple. "See how she bleeds. A witch cannot bleed! By God's Holy Mother, I'll kill the man who did this!"

The beggars had no stomach for murder. Stoning a witch was fair sport, but now they were uncertain. Turning, they ran from the gates, each one eager to be gone from Aldbridge before they could be accused. The rain dripped on the bruised white face and Kit and Jeffrey stood alone and faced each other.

"God damn you, Kit Wakeman!" Jeffrey spat out the words. "Devil take you for a liar!"

"I had to say it, Jeffrey. She knew about the cause, and the beggars heard what she tried to say. I did it for the cause, Jeffrey. And for Mary Stuart."

Slowly with hatred sparkling in his eyes, Jeffrey spoke.

"Then damn your cause, Kit Wakeman. And the devil take Mary Stuart. I want no part in it now!"

Gently he bent down and moved Meg's cloak from the mud over which it had billowed. The sight of her body shocked him. Incredulously he raised his eyes from her distorted swollen form.

"Is this your doing, and all?" he whispered bitterly.

Tenderly he lifted Meg in his strong young arms, and carried her home.

TEN

" HELP ME," called Meg, " they will kill me! Help me, Kit!"

They were throwing gooseberries at her; gooseberries big as cobblestones, and Kit stood and mocked. She was dreaming. Soon she would waken and her mother would be holding her tightly. She struggled against the blackness.

" Mother?"

" I am here, little bird." The dear, safe voice called her from the nightmare. " Lie still. 'Tis all over now. You are safe."

Meg opened her eyes, Lord, how her head hurt. She held out her arms for comfort as she always did.

" It was the dream again. They threw gooseberries." Meg blinked her eyes. She could not see properly. Kit was bending over her, but his body was shifting like a reflection on a wind-rippled pool.

" Kit?" Meg held out her hand. " You have come for me?"

A strong hand enfolded Meg's and held it tight.

" It is Jeffrey, Meg."

" Jeffrey?"

The mists cleared, and Meg closed her eyes again. Kit had not come.

"Can you stand, little one?" Gently Jeffrey cradled her throbbing head in the crook of his arm.

Meg shook her head. Now she remembered. She had not been dreaming. She had run to Kit and he had called her a witch! She had tried to tell him about the baby, but he hadn't understood. The acrid smell of the burning feather Goody waved beneath Meg's nose caused her eyes to water.

"Leave me be, Goody. It is all right, I can stand, now."

She held out her hands for help, and tenderly Jeffrey lifted her from the floor, as easily as if she were a small child. Meg looked at her swollen body.

"See my shame, Jeffrey. Now the whole village must know," she whispered bitterly.

"No, Meg. No one else knows but Kit Wakeman, and then only when I lifted aside your cloak. Sir Crispin's men were gone and the beggars fled."

Gently he helped her to the staircase.

"You are good to me, Jeffrey. If only I could love you," Meg gave him a sad little smile, "but it is too late, even if I were willing to try. It is no use now."

Stiffly, for her whole body ached, Meg climbed to her room.

"There now, my pretty. Nurse will bathe your poor wounded head and give you a sleeping posset. It will all seem better in the morning."

Gently Goody helped Meg's clumsy efforts at undressing.

" Silly bairn, running out into the storm, and frightening us half to death!"

Anne brought linen bandages and marshmallow salve.

" Poor little Meg," the midwife soothed. " Goody will bind your head."

Gratefully Meg lay back on the bed.

" It is not my head that needs binding. 'Tis my back. Lord, the pains shoot down it and into my belly. Rub my back, Goody."

Anne's eyes met Goody's. *So,* they signalled, *it is to be a birthday babe, after all!*

John stared ahead to the furthest tip of the cow pasture.

" You say, Jeffrey, that Kit Wakeman knows of Meg's babe?"

" Aye, Master Weaver. He was surprised as I was. I know it, for it showed in his face."

The two men leaned on the gate by the rowan tree. The storm was over and the scent of rain-soaked greenery hung sweet on the evening air.

" And would you think, Jeffrey, that apart from the two of you, no one knows?"

" I would swear to it, sir. I did not guess until I pulled Meg's cloak aside to lift her. It had billowed about her as she fell, and hid her body. No one else could have known, for only Kit Wakeman and I were there. All others had fled."

John's fingertips drummed on the gate. " Did any see you as you brought her home?"

" I think not, Master Weaver. The villagers had shuttered their windows and barred their doors. Meg's secret is safe."

D*

" Now you know why Meg has seemed so mettlesome these past months, and asked you not to see her." John looked at his fingertips, reluctant to meet Jeffrey's eyes. " We put about lies so that the village may not know. Mistress Weaver wishes to claim the child as her own. We did what we thought was best. We did not seek to deceive you, Jeffrey."

" We all do what we think to be best. Only time tells us whether we have been right or not." Jeffrey shrugged his shoulders. " Meg thought it best when she told Kit that you knew of his secret. Had she held her peace he would not have accused her of witchcraft. I saw Meg as I sheltered in the wood. She cried as she ran, and called Kit Wakeman's name, so I followed her. Would to God I had got to her sooner."

" You did what you could, Jeffrey. I am in your debt."

" Then if that is so, sir, I ask that you let Meg and I wed."

John looked into the anxious face beside him. " Would you want her, Jeffrey, knowing that at this moment she labours with another's child?"

" What does it matter? Who knows of it save ourselves? All the village believe it is Mistress Weaver who is with child. My mother prays each night for her safe delivery. If Meg would have me I will wed her gladly. I love her, and I think she would come to love me."

" God's Truth, you are a good lad, Jeffrey. Only give Meg a chance to forget Kit. She will have the babe at her breast for a time, but if you will wait, I know she will come to you."

" I will wait, Master Weaver, though times are trouble-some. I pray I will be spared."

" Spared? You speak mortal strange for one so young."

" Do not fox with me, Master Weaver. You know of the plotting hereabouts. How else would Meg have known of it?"

John remembered the night he had returned from the Manor. Meg had been awake. She must have heard all. It would be useless to deny it.

" I know there is a plot to take Elizabeth Tudor's throne for Mary Stuart. Do you also know of it, Jeffrey?"

" Aye, sir, I know of it right well, for I am pledged to it. And my father and elder brother, also."

" God's Blood, where will the folly of it end? Do they wish to set families at variance and split England apart?"

John's body shook with anger. Could not men leave well alone? Had they forgotten the screams of the tortured who would not acknowledge Henry Tudor's divorce? Had the sickening smell of burning Protestants been forgotten like a bad dream when Mary Tudor died? Elizabeth wanted only what was best for England. She had given years of peace to her kingdom.

" Is your religion so important to you that you would shed blood for it, Jeffrey? There can only be one heaven. Does it matter how we pray our way into it?"

" Sir, I am confused. I would not deny Meg's beliefs for I know she cleaves to the Anglican church. Will you not respect mine?"

There was much sense in the young, thought John, and he clasped Jeffrey's hand in his.

" You shame me, lad. I will say no more on the matter.

I only pray that nothing will come of the plotting, for it would mean civil war in the land. I do not agree with what you seek to do, but I shall not betray you."

John looked upwards to the lighted window of the bedchamber.

"Go home, Jeffrey. It is useless to wait. Meg's labours might last long into the night. One more favour I would ask of you. 'Tis certain that talk will get about of this day's happening's. I think I can bargain with Kit to hold his peace about Meg's child, but servants were there when she was accused of witchcraft. If she is openly charged, will you tell what you saw in her defence?"

"That I will, Master Weaver. But none will believe Meg a witch when I swear that she bled when she was stoned. Nothing would come of such a charge, I am certain." Jeffrey raised his hand in salute. "I bid you goodnight, sir. God guard your house this night."

From where John sat at the foot of the loft staircase, he heard a low moan of pain, then all was quiet.

"God's Holy Mother, help my Meg," he whispered.

In the little garret room, Meg Weaver held tightly to her mother's hand.

"Gently, little one," soothed Goody, "be still if you can. The babe is all but born. Gently, now."

A pain, jagged and terrible, tore at Meg's body, pulling her limb from limb, numbing her senses and choking the cry that arose in her throat. Viciously it possessed her, enveloped her in its blackness, and devoured her.

"Kit!" she called, as though with her last breath.

"'Tis over!" Goody gave a sob of triumph. "Thank God, 'tis over!"

Quickly she bit through the umbilical cord, and deftly tied it. Holding the child by its ankles she slapped its buttocks and thighs.

"Now, my beauty," she whispered, hooking her little finger into the tiny mouth. "Come now, little one."

The child spluttered and gasped, coughing the life-giving air into its lungs. Then angrily protesting, it bawled itself into life.

"God be praised!" cried Goody. "We have a fine healthy boy!"

Sitting by the fire, the baby on her lap, Anne gently rubbed the little body with sweet almond oil and wrapped it in bands of swaddling linen.

"He is so beautiful," she whispered, "so wondrous fair."

Cradling him in her arms she marvelled at his perfection.

"We have a fine child," she smiled at John through happy tears.

Gently John touched the little hand.

"'Tis almost like when Meg was born," he said. "I feel the same joy surging through me."

"And so you should, husband," Anne teased, "for is he not your son? Do not forget, John, this babe is *ours*." Joyously, Anne rocked the child in her arms. "I do not care what lies we have told, nor who we have deceived. This sweet creature has made it all worth while. Oh, John! How they will envy us our son when we carry him out. I'll swear I feel young enough to have borne him myself!"

John looked at the flushed cheeks and shining eyes of his wife. He had not seen such gladness in her face for many a day. How then could this deception be wrong? The child would be known as John Weaver's son, and none could point the finger at him. In time Meg and Jeffrey would marry. They were young. There would be other babies for Meg. Anne was content, looking as all women did when they held a new-born child; beautiful beyond measure. A few lies did not matter . . .

Goody Trewitt stumped into the room and sat by the fire.

" I have lost count of the babes I have brought into this world, yet still I thrill to it. And you, mistress, must be abed tomorrow. 'Tis going to take the guile of a fox to sort out this kettle of fish! I am greatly feared," she smiled wickedly at Anne, " that your sickly condition will not allow you visitors for many days!"

John laid his arm round the bent old shoulders.

" One day, Goody Trewitt, I will repay your goodness," he promised.

How wonderful, thought Anne, to have a baby by the hearth again. When her pretended lying-in was over and the need for deception gone, she would be able to walk out with the child in her arms. Tomorrow, Anne decided, Goody must carry him to church for Father Sedgwick to baptise.

" Meg, little maid," Anne bent over her daughter, " here is your babe, crying with hunger. Hold him close and give him your breast."

Meg held out her arms. " He is mine, yet I cannot own him. I got a love-child, and I must give him to you." Tenderly she guided the searching mouth to her nipple. " But this only I, his mother, can do for him." Softly she brushed her lips over the fair down on the little head.

" In all else, madam, he is yours. I give him to you gladly.
I give him for your goodness, and beg that you forgive me."

" Silly cuckoo!" Anne's voice was rough with emotion.
" Cease your nonsense this instant, or you'll curdle your
milk!"

ELEVEN

" WHY WILL Father Sedgwick not come? Did you tell him, Jeffrey, that Mistress Trewitt said Meg was in dire need of a priest?"

" Aye, madam, I did, but Father Sedgwick has heard the whispers of witchcraft that are passed about the village. He says he will not come to Meg until these stories have been proved false. She is an accused witch, and he cannot give her absolution."

" Then may God damn him for a turncoat priest!" Anne fought back her sobs. " Must my Meg die without the benefit of the church?"

Now, at sundown, it seemed a far cry from the early hours of the morning when they had been so happy. Goody had first noticed Meg's pallor.

" I do not like it," she confided to John. " She sleeps too much. A young maid should throw off her labour with no trouble at all. She was hit about the head yesterday, and there I think lies the root of the trouble. Still, there is no need to say anything of this to Anne yet a while."

But Anne had been quick to comment on the ugly bruise that spread from Meg's temple.

" Damn him who threw that stone!" She had not been able to contain her bitterness. " And damn the one who called her witch!"

" Come, Anne, Meg will soon perk up," Goody comforted. " She has suffered much these last months. We must not expect too much, too soon."

" I am not impatient, but it is frightful strange to me that when I took the babe to Meg again, she did not want him. I am mortal afraid, Goody. All is not well, and I blame the blow to her head. I have seen strong men die of such bruising. They say it can addle the brain."

" Stop your fretting, Anne Weaver," Goody spoke roughly. " Meet trouble when it comes knocking on your door, and then only if you must."

Nevertheless, the midwife had been forced to concede that all was not well. Now, with the passing of the hours, Meg lay like a quiet little ghost, the moving of her lips the only sign that life still existed in the pale still body.

" Bid Jeffrey fetch Father Sedgwick. I do not like her mutterings," Goody had said. " She whispers that she is a flower reborn. I fear for her, Anne. Such ramblings come only from the dying."

But Jeffrey had told them that Father Sedgwick was loath to leave his supper table.

" God damn him!" cried Anne again. " And what of the babe? What is to be done, Goody?"

" Hush your wailing," clucked Goody. " There is nothing to be done, for we cannot drag him protesting from his victuals if he chooses not to come, though may his food stick in his gullet and choke him!"

" I will go myself," Anne made for the door. " He will listen to me. He will not refuse a mother's pleadings."

" He can, and he will. Father Sedgwick is afraid of his own shadow. All married priests are alike." Goody spat into the fire. " Remember, Anne, that you are confined to your bed. You must not walk out. I'll baptise the child for you, though. At least the babe shall not suffer."

" How can you baptise a bairn?"

Goody stared into the fire, seeming not to have heard what Anne had asked. Then slowly, without shifting her eyes, she spoke.

" Because, God forgive me, I was once a nun." She took a gulp of the ale she held in her hand. " Does it surprise you, Anne? And you, Jeffrey?"

" Why did you not tell me, Goody?" Anne begged the question. " We have been friends for almost a score years, yet you said nothing."

" I said nothing," Goody looked from Anne to Jeffrey, " and I charge you both to keep your peace. I came from the nunnery of St. Clement, in York. When Henry Tudor turned on the church, it was not only the monasteries he closed. I went with the Mother Prioress to lodgings in Trinity street. Sir Crispin's father took pity on me and found me a home. I came to my little house in Aldbridge, and I have nursed the sick here ever since."

" What can I say, Goody! I pity you with all my heart," Anne's voice trembled.

" Pity me, Anne Weaver? God's Wounds, I do not want your pity! It was the happiest day of my life when Henry Tudor unlocked my prison gates, aye, and paid me a pension into the bargain!" Goody chuckled at the disbelief on the faces of her listeners. " I was fat, Anne; fat and ugly, and no man would take me to wed. I was an encumbrance to my family, so my father paid my dowry to the church and lo and behold, I was wed to Christ! 'Twas a fearsome life, locked away from the sight of all but the sick. Those nuns were bitches, all of them, that I tell you. They quivered for the sight of a man. And God! there were more fastdays than feastdays. I was right glad to turn my back on it. 'Twas a fair wind that blew me to Aldbridge."

Goody rolled up her sleeves, enjoying the consternation she had caused.

" 'Tis a long time since I baptised a babe. I did not renounce my vows—Harry Tudor, the old stallion, did that, not I, so the good God will not quarrel with what I do. Would I could give absolution to Meg, but that was never in my power. The babe is different, though. He has no sin upon him. Give him to me, Anne, and fetch a bowl of water from the rain butt. The sooner it is done, the sooner I can away and give Master Sedgwick a piece of my mind!"

Goody laid the child on her arm, and splashed his head with water.

" It is not holy water, Anne, but it has dropped from the heavens, so 'tis the next best thing."

She signed the tiny forehead with a cross and blessed his lips and his heart.

" Sweet babe," Goody kissed the top of his head, " I name thee Harry, in the name of the Father, the Son, and the Holy Ghost."

" Amen," said Anne and Jeffrey, and blessed themselves.

Goody handed the baby back to Anne. " Do not ask me why I christened him so. Perhaps it was in gratitude to him who gave me my freedom. Now, I'll away and say my piece to that good-for-nothing priest!"

Before she could lift the latch, there was an urgent hammering on the door.

" Thank God!" Anne ran to welcome the caller. " I knew Father Sedgwick would come to Meg."

But Father Sedgwick had not repented. It was Kit Wakeman who stood at the door.

The cry of welcome died on Anne's lips.

" So, Master Kit, you are come to see your bastard?" she spat out the words bitterly. " You have fathered a fine son, my proud young cock! Thank God you will never be able to own him!"

" Anne love, hush your rantings!" Quietly John Weaver motioned to the pale-faced youth. " Come in, young master. There is nothing to be gained from bandying words on the door-stone." Gently he closed the door. " Young sir, my station in life forbids me the pleasure of giving you the whipping you deserve. Still, I say this to you. Few know of Meg's baby. Mistress Weaver and myself will bring him up as our son. Now you know that the child my wife expected was an invention, spread about so that Meg might not suffer." John spoke quietly and deliberately, his eyes cold and hard. " But if you utter one word of what you have learned, I promise you on God's Life you will live to regret it, for I too have learned of something it were best should not be known. Do you understand my meaning, Kit Wakeman?"

" Aye, John Weaver, your meaning is plain to me." He

scuffed the floor with his foot, uneasily. "I will give you my hand on it, and my word as a gentleman."

"God, Kit Wakeman," hissed Goody, "do you know the meaning of such a word? By Christ's Wounds, young *gentleman*, I wish with all my heart it had been your head I slapped when I brought you into the world, and not your backside! Perhaps I'd have knocked some sense into it, and some arrogance out!"

John held up his hand. "Hush your mouth, Goody. Slinging words like arrows will help no one. Do you come to see Meg, Master Wakeman?"

"He shall not see her," sobbed Anne, eyes blazing. "Nor the child! Think you to use my maid as you would use a whore? Would you spoil her, then creep into my house to beg her forgiveness. By God, you shall not have it, Kit Wakeman! Lie with your guilty conscience beside you on your pillow to torment you. It will make a poor bed-fellow!"

"Anne!" John Weaver shook his wife's arm. "Master Wakeman is our visitor, and I invited him over my threshold. I ask you to treat him as such. He shall see Meg. I will take him to her."

In the darkened little room, Meg lay still and white on the bed. Shocked and penitent, Kit dropped to his knees beside her.

"Meg," he whispered. "Meg, little sweeting, it is Kit."

The pale lips moved. "Kit?"

"Meg, dear heart, I meant you no wrong. Forgive me." Taking her hand he laid it to his lips. "Forgive your Kit. I cannot live in peace with my conscience if you do not."

Desperately she turned to John. " She will not open her eyes. What ails her?"

" She is in her death sleep. Not all your pleadings will rouse her. It is best that you leave. You must seek your absolution elsewhere," John Weaver's voice trembled. " Get you gone from my house. Meg cannot ease the sins of your soul."

" Meg, little love," Kit cried, " if ever you loved me, speak to me and say I am forgiven."

Almost imperceptibly, Meg moved her head, released for a few brief seconds from her stupor.

" Kit." Her eyes flickered open and met his. " I will come again." The words were barely a whisper. " One day, in some other life, I will have you. Wherever you are, I will find you."

" Meg, you speak to me! Now say you will forgive your Kit?"

But Meg did not hear the anguished pleading, for her moment of wakefulness was gone.

" It is no use. There is no sense in what she says."

John knelt by Meg's bed and gently took her hand in his own.

The harvest moon sailed high in the September sky, and still John knelt in vigil. There was a movement of Meg's fingers within John's hand like the fluttering heart of a frightened bird, and he laid her hand to his cheek.

" Kit, love, remember . . ."

Afraid he might miss Meg's whispered words, John held his breath.

". . . never step on a heartsease lest you hurt your Meg. Tread not on a heartsease, Kit."

And holding the hand she believed to be Kit's, Meg Weaver died.

"God forgive you, Kit Wakeman," whispered Goody Trewitt. "God forgive you, for I never shall."

Gently she dressed Meg in the dress she had loved so much, her first dress of womanhood with the heartsease sewn around the neck. Sweet Jesus, who could call this beautiful broken child a witch? Her body was perfect with never a devil's mark to be found on it. The last time Meg had worn her woman's dress, she had danced with the Lord of Misrule with the love in her eyes for all to see, aye, and danced too well to his tune, no doubt, for surely it was then she had got herself with child.

Goody laid Meg's arms by her sides and took the pillow from beneath her head. By the bed lay the cere-cloth. She must wrap the waxed winding-sheet round the cold little body, for those who are refused Christian burial have little use for shrouds or coffins.

"Sweet little love, you were the fairest babe I ever brought into the world."

Goody contorted her face and squeezed her eyelids tight. She would not weep. Tears were a luxury she could ill afford this day. Slowly she climbed down the loft staircase.

"Go to her now." Goody laid her arm round Anne's shoulders. "I have laid her straight and true. Do not touch her."

By the hearth, John stood transfixed, loath to enter the room where Meg lay.

"I will away now, good John, for the babe needs sustenance, and I must find a wet-nurse for him. When it

is dark, you must lay Meg in the earth." She took John's
arm and shook it, for he seemed deaf to her words. " Do
you heed what I say? It must be done secretly, and none
must know where she rests. Not even Anne. If none know,
then none can defile her grave."

John nodded blankly.

" Think on what I have told you. *Anne must not know.*
It is the best way."

Then she went out into the solace of the soft night, and
shed the tears that could no longer be denied.

It was well, thought Goody, as she straightened her
shoulders at last, and hobbled towards the inn, that when
one door closed, another would surely open. She had
always been reluctant to give a draft that would take away
the milk from a woman's breasts, for there was always a
demand for a good wet-nurse.

Stupid Polly, the inn-keeper's daughter, had eaten
richly these last three years when God in His wisdom
willed that her babies be stillborn. It was wondered how
Polly got herself with child so often, but being an inn-
keeper's daughter and simple, it wasn't all that much of a
miracle, decided Goody. Two days ago, Polly had had yet
another dead child, and now her breasts would be hard
with unsucked milk. So far as Goody knew, no woman in
the district was in need of a wet-nurse; and with luck
Polly's milk would still be available.

It was with relief that Goody found the simple girl
sitting by her father's hearth, hugging her aching breasts
and wailing for her dead baby.

" It is for poor Mistress Weaver's babe that I ask it,"
Goody told the inn-keeper. " The shock of Meg's death

has robbed her of her milk. Her babe will starve."

" Take the silly strumpet. Take her and welcome. Well rid I am of her. 'Twill be one mouth less to feed," he said, accepting the silver crown Goody pressed into his hand.

" She will be well cared for," promised Goody. " None shall take advantage of her simplicity whilst she is in Mistress Weaver's care."

She walked over to the crying girl, and shook her shoulder.

" Come with me, Polly. I know of a hungry babe who needs your milk. Will you nurse him?"

The girl smiled and nodded. Tears forgotten, she followed Goody gladly.

TWELVE

CLOSE TO the stone-pit, where the road to Ripon crossed the old Roman way to York, John Weaver beat down the last clod of earth. By these crossroads the invaders of a thousand years ago had hewn out the red sandstone blocks to build their walls and pave their streets. Now the stone-pit was unused. None would look for a grave hereabouts. The freshly disturbed earth could easily be disguised by a covering of rubble.

One day perhaps, John would tell Anne where Meg lay. Now in her grief, it was kinder that she should not know. John's mind was still numb and it was better so. How else could he have given Meg to the earth? How else, when villagers called at his house, could he have kept up the pretence of the near-miracle of Anne's newborn son?

There had been much sympathy for them at Meg's death. Some had openly condemned Kit Wakeman for his accusation, for they could not understand his reason for making it. Meg's death, they said, must weigh heavily on his conscience. Some had found Father Sedgwick wanting for his refusal to take Meg into the church for Christian burial.

But there had been gladness for them at the birth of their son, and they had sent Anne their greetings and promised prayers for Meg. Now it could only be a matter of time, John knew, before Sir Crispin would have to face him, for Sir Crispin must find out how much of what Meg had told Kit was truth, and how much the hysterical fancies of a young girl.

What would he do, thought John, when the time of confrontation came? He had wanted to forget what he had overheard. He could not believe those men could turn traitor. Even now he was not sure he could betray them. Jeffrey was pledged to the cause. Could John place a rope around Jeffrey's neck? If only Elizabeth Tudor had not given sanctuary to the Scottish Queen.

Walter Skelton had sensed evil, and warned of it, but John had not listened. What would Walter make of all this? thought John. Walter would travel to London with the speed of the wind and warn the Queen of the danger. But who would care for Anne and the babe if *he* were to do that, mused John. How long would it take him to travel to London? How would a humble farmer seek an audience with a Queen?

John blew out his lantern and made for home, his mind in a turmoil. There were noblemen in York from the Court in London who sat on the Queen's Council of the North. Those men would be loyal to Elizabeth Tudor. Would they listen to what he had to tell? Would they believe it if they did listen? John knew he could not discuss the matter with Anne. She must not be involved. Betrayal was a man's work. He must go to York, and find Walter. Walter would know what was to be done, or whether it would be wisest to wait and say nothing. His mind made up, John opened his kitchen door.

Anne knelt by the hearth, rocking gently in her misery. Her eyes were swollen with weeping, and she did not speak as John walked towards her. In the ingle sat Polly, a smile on her vacant face, with Meg's babe at her breast. A great bitterness shot through John's heart like a savage pain. Damn them all and their plotting! Meg had been their first victim. Where would it end? How many more innocents must die?

Suddenly John wanted revenge. He cared nothing if he were truthful for the Queen's safety or for those who lived around him; or whether prayers were chanted in Latin, or spoken in English. Meg was dead, and England could run with blood for all he cared if that would bring her back.

"Go to bed, Anne," he said, his voice rough with emotion, "and sleep Polly and the babe in Meg's room. I'm away to York. If I leave now, I shall be there by morning."

"To York, John? At this hour? Why must you travel with such pressing haste? The roads are unsafe at night with footpads, and the beggars are still afoot."

"I must seek out Walter Skelton. That is all you need to know. Should any come looking for me, especially Sir Crispin, tell them I have gone to Ripon on weaving business."

"But that would be a lie, John, and you have never lied in your life."

"Then I am of a mind to begin. I charge you, Anne, say nothing of where I have gone. What you do not know cannot harm you." John took his stave from behind the door. " Give me a kiss, love."

Anne laid her cheek near his. It was useless to try to stop John when his mind was made up, and anyway, she had no spirit left in her to try.

" God go with you," she whispered.

That night, long-tailed buzzards and creeping things in hedge-bottoms steered a course clear of John as he strode the road to York. Even Lucifer himself would have trodden warily had he met him, so black with hatred was John Weaver's soul.

The sun had warmed away the early September chill from the wide street of Micklegate when John entered the city of York. His walk through the night had rid him of the demons that tormented him. Once more his conscience walked by his side, and he was again loath to betray men amongst whom he lived and worked. But bitterness against those whose plotting had caused Meg's death flowed from him like a torrent.

Meg is dead! How often during the night had he said those words, beating them into his brain to convince himself it had happened, that he was not walking through a black dream from which he would soon awaken to find his sweet Meg laughing by his side.

Under the arch of the great bar at Micklegate streamed farmers and millers, tinkers and bakers, each making his way to the market place to sell or barter his goods. John walked aimlessly, letting the pushing crowd take him with them. Even now he was not sure of what was best to do. But Walter would help him. Walter knew the ways of the world, and would know what was to be done.

The stench of the slaughterhouses and the putrefying waste thrown from the butchers' shops in the Shambles made John retch. He stood still, inhaling the foul air and gulping it into his belly. The whole street stank of death and decay. It was what life was made of and John wanted to be a part of it. He wanted to feel so vile inside him that betrayal would come easily. He squared his shoulders and made for Petergate.

"Beg pardon, sir!"

A young apprentice turned the corner looking over his shoulder as he ran. The force of his body as it crashed into John's sent them both tumbling to the gutter.

"I'm sorry, master. I did not look where I ran." Anxiously the boy scrambled to his feet, and held out a helping hand to John. "Your cap is scarce marked."

The boy rubbed it with his sleeve before handing it back to John. The lad reminded him, thought John, of the days of his own apprenticeship. Doubtless the lad had been sent on an errand by his master and had dawdled in the sunshine, or stolen a few minutes with some little serving maid. How often had John done the same when Anne had worked in Trinity Lane, in the town house of Sir Crispin's parents?

"Be off with you, young jackanapes."

The boy fled like the wind. He was not unlike Jeffrey. Jeffrey was a good lad and pledged to Mary Stuart's cause. But how easy would it be to betray one who had loved Meg?

The servant at the Cloth Merchant's house said Master Skelton had left for Lincoln in the early spring and would not be back in York until Michaelmas. John closed his eyes wearily. He had not expected Walter to be away. He had relied on the help and good council his old friend would give him. Walter's absence was yet another blow to John's reeling senses. There was no one now to whom he could turn. The decision would have to be his alone. Maybe it were better so, then only he would have to answer to his conscience, and to God.

John had not thought of God. Suddenly he remembered the little church of St. Mary where he had prayed each Sunday as a boy, walking solemnly behind his master with the other apprentices from their lodgings in Felter Lane. He would go there again and try to find the peace he had known in his youth. He would pray as he had prayed then, asking St. Zita to help him. St. Zita had been his patron saint. Would she remember him? It was a long time since he had asked for her intercession.

He did not enter the church as intended, for a beggar woman barred his way.

" Help a poor woman, good sir?" She held out her bowl. " Pinch the idiot and see her dance. One penny to pinch the idiot, sir."

" Aye, master," urged a woman who stood beside them, " she'll get mortal vicious when you pinch her backside. 'Tis better than cock-fighting when she does her mad dance. Be sporty, good sir. Give us all a laugh to ease our empty bellies."

The idiot girl, chained to the railings of the churchyard, crouched like a whipped dog, her arms wrapped round her head.

John took a coin from his purse. " Here is a penny, but I charge you to buy bread for the maid with it. Leave the creature in peace. I do not want entertainment today."

" Nay, good sir, you have paid for your amusement and you shall have it." The old woman gave the girl a pinch. " Dance for your dinner, my pretty. See, sir, how she rages. Is it not a fine show?"

The girl responded to the pinch as she had been taught. Stupid as she was, she knew that if she did not there would be a strap about her shoulders. Running her fingers through her matted hair she glowered at those about her, jumping about like a caged wild creature. Angrily she shook her fist at those who mocked her, grunting animal noises, and slobbering like a baby. Then she thumbed her filthy nose and turned her bare backside to the crowd exactly as she knew she must. The entertainment was over, as the idiot crouched by the railings once more.

John swallowed hard on the vomit that rose in his throat. He remembered again—Meg was dead. He had laid her unblessed in the cold earth and marked her grave with rubble. He would never again wonder at her pale beauty or watch the firelight gentle her face as she dreamed by the hearth. Yet this creature of degradation that crouched at his feet lived. God's Holy Blood, was there no end to what a man must bear? *Meg is dead and this animal lives!* The words screamed inside his head. Christ's Wounds, someone must pay! And the vileness inside him burned like a fire and clutched at his belly like a pain of hell.

Now he knew beyond all doubt, what he must do.

John looked up to the fortified Bar and remembered Walter Skelton's words. It was easy now, he thought, to understand the journeyman's reasons for seeking the shelter of the city walls. A man could feel safer and sleep easier with such massive protection about him.

From the watch towers set high in the turrets, a sentry might gaze out far beyond the forest that gave shelter to wild deer and swine to open country that stretched wild to the northern horizon. Those men who manned the walls at Bootham saw most of the fighting in times of stress, for it was from there the alarm had sounded in times past when danger swept down from the Pennines and the Scottish Marches.

Still uncertain, John loitered in the courtyard of the King's Manor. It was an ordinary house—no bigger than Sir Crispin's home at Aldbridge. It seemed strange that to this manor King Henry once brought Catherine, his Queen. Dimly John remembered the excitement and bustle when it was made known that the King would visit the city with his beautiful young bride. It seemed stranger that after all the months of preparation, very few had seen either the King or his Queen.

" Too taken up with his fine new filly to show himself to the common folk," one of the older apprentices had exclaimed to John; but for all that, King Henry's wanton young queen had been dragged screaming to her execution little more than a year later.

John thought back to the bloody and tempestuous days of his youth. He had known the uncertainty and fears of a land torn by religious torment. He remembered the upheaval of the old religion at odds with Henry Tudor's new church. And after the death of the sickly Edward, the Protestant realm he left behind him was turned topsy-turvy by his half-sister Catholic Mary, and the burning

E

of heretics had begun. Those who would not recant and turn once more to Rome had known the hellfires at Smithfield.

The more unhappy the barren Mary had become, the more the stench of burning flesh had filled the air of London. Then, at last, came Elizabeth, bringing with her the calm England John now knew. She had been fair to all men, whether they profesed the old faith or the new. There had followed ten years of peace and plenty, and many had cause to bless her, even those who called her bastard.

Now the good years were to be swept away because one who had been hounded from her Scottish Kingdom schemed with Spain to take the throne of her protector, and misguided Englishmen plotted to bring back the rule of Rome and turn traitor to the most gracious ruler on the face of God's earth.

THIRTEEN

" Ho, there!" called the trooper who stood sentry by the heavy oak door, his cry jerking John to earth again. " Why do you hang about? Advance and state your business, or be on your way."

John turned and walked slowly and reluctantly towards the soldier. His mind was a torment of doubts, and he was still loath to set the seal on his act of betrayal. But had not Kit betrayed Meg, and in doing, caused her death? And Sir Crispin, Kit's father, plotted to overthrow the crowned Queen of the land, and set brother against brother for the sake of a foreign Pope.

John dropped his head, reluctant to look even at an unknown trooper. Nervously he tugged at his belt. His hands were still soiled from his labours of the previous night. Was it only a few short hours since Meg had lain there and pitfully gasped for Kit? For Kit who sought with the rest of his ilk to take more innocent lives so that their consciences might rest easier in heaven. John squared his shoulders.

" My business is with Lord Sussex," he said clearly, for he said it for Meg.

The sentry had seen John's like before. Always those men who asked to see the Earl of Sussex acted in such a way. They would dawdle in the courtyard, or stand in the shadow of the stables, uncertain maybe, or afraid of being seen. Always their business was with the Earl and always, for some reason, the Earl found time to talk to them.

There had been great activity of late at the King's Manor. Queen's messengers had arrived almost daily, and men with Scottish accents had been given a safe conduct to the Borders when their business with Lord Sussex was done.

It was said that the Queen of Scotland was the cause of the commotion. It was common talk in the city taverns that the Council had met in York on the orders of the Queen of England to clear the name of Mary Stuart and declare her innocent of any dealings in her husband's murder. And when the Scottish Queen's innocence had been proved, men said that Elizabeth Tudor would journey to York, and warmly embrace the cousin to whom she had given refuge.

The sentry sighed. Now here was another to see the Earl of Sussex. Lord, he thought, as he stamped his weary feet, the sooner his stint with the Militia was over, the quicker he could be back to his anvil.

"Lord Sussex, is it?" The sentry jerked his thumb over his shoulder. "Well, you'll have to see Sir Ralph Sadler first. You only see his lordship if Sir Ralph thinks you will. Knock on yonder door. The clerk will attend to you."

"I am grateful to you, sir."

John nodded his head and walked towards the half-open

door by the stables. There could be no going back now.

The pock-marked clerk laid down his quill and shuffled off, grumbling, in search of Sir Ralph Sadler.

"Likely he'll not see you," he muttered over his shoulder. "He's powerful busy, these days."

But Sir Ralph nevertheless made himself available, knowing that mention of the Duke of Alva made it imperative he should speak with the man who would not give his name.

"We can talk privately now," he said, closing the door behind him, "but first you must give me your name, good fellow."

"I am John Weaver, sir, a yeoman from Aldbridge, twenty miles to the north-east of this city."

"I know it well." Sir Ralph nodded and pulled a chair to the table, indicating that John do likewise. "And how does Aldbridge concern me and the Duke of Alva, Master Weaver?"

"Because, sir, at the home of Sir Crispin Wakeman, the name of the Duke of Alva was mentioned."

"You are sure it was the Duke of Alva?"

"I am sure."

John spoke quietly and firmly. He had cast the first stone; the rest now would be easy.

"It is not a sin for Sir Crispin to mention the name of the Duke of Alva. The Duke is a high-ranking Spanish nobleman. Many have heard of him."

"I had not, sir, until last night."

Sir Ralph fingered his beard thoughtfully. It was unlikely the man could have made up the name, he reasoned.

" How did you hear the Duke of Alva's name mentioned? Were you present at the time?"

" No, sir, but I stood outside the room in which they all sat. I was not mistaken."

" They? Give me the names of the men who were in the room."

For a moment John hesitated.

" There was Sir Richard Norton and two of his sons; and Stormcock Tempest and Tankard from Borough-bridge," he said at last. " There was also Sir Crispin Wakeman, and his son, Kit."

" You would swear to this?"

" I would swear."

Sir Ralph wrote down the names he had been given.

" And why do you think it should be of interest to the Earl of Sussex that men should gather at Aldbridge and mention the name of the Duke of Alva?"

" Because they also mentioned the name *Marie*, and I know full well that the Marie they spoke of is the one who was lodged at Bolton."

" And what other names were mentioned?" The story the weaver told was beginning to make sense, now, thought Sir Ralph Sadler. " Can you remember any other names?"

" Aye, Sir Ralph, they spoke of de Spes, or so it sounded."

" They could have spoken in innocence, Master Weaver. If the Earl of Sussex were to summon these men to York to give an account to the Council of their meeting, they could swear it was only gossip that had transpired between them."

John raised his eyes to those of his questioner.

" It could have been gossip, but I would swear that it was not. Why else would the carter travel from Northumberland with a load of sea-coal? It is likely the sea-coal covered arms, for there was talk of arms and armour being sent from the Earl of Northumberland. The men who sat with Sir Crispin spoke of where they had hidden those arms in their homes. And they said that when the bells rang out, they would also take the levy arms from their churches."

The man was becoming uneasy. He knew the men the weaver had mentioned, and knew that without a doubt they were all loyal to the old faith. And it was certain, too, that to couple the names of Alva and de Spes with Mary Stuart left a riddle that only the Earl of Sussex was competent to untangle.

" Tell me one more thing, and on your honour, Master Weaver. Why have you travelled to York to tell me these things?"

For a moment John stared at his hands. His mouth was dry and he almost hated himself for what he was doing. But the soil from the stone quarry still clung to his fingers, and he was reminded of why it was there. Clearly and carefully he told his story.

At the house where once the Abbot of St. Mary's had lived and which men now called the King's Manor, Thomas Radcliffe, Earl of Sussex, sat at his dinner table and twirled the stem of the fine glass goblet between his finger and thumb.

" What did you think of Master Weaver, Ralph?"

Ralph Sadler stood by the great window and looked out to where the afternoon sun touched the old stones of the

Bar at Bootham and mellowed the golden towers of the great Minster. The story John Weaver told had saddened and alarmed him. He had not wanted to believe it, yet common sense told him he must.

"I think," he said, "he is an honest man."

"And would you say his words were to be trusted?"

Sir Ralph thought for a moment before answering. "The man did not speak of love for his Queen or his country. He spoke only of revenge against those who had harmed his daughter. He asked neither favour or reward. I would trust him."

"I am inclined to agree with you, Ralph. Revenge was ever a more reliable motive for betrayal that patriotism. Grief and bitterness often loosen a man's tongue. Tomorrow when it is too late, Master Weaver will regret what he has done."

Sir Ralph walked to the table and refilled his goblet. "If what Master Weaver tells us is true, it could mean civil war in the land. It would set houses apart, and north against south. And do you know, my Lord Sussex, this city of York still beats with a Catholic heart?"

"Aye, Ralph, I know it. Some men would cast away ten years of peace for a foreign Pope." Sussex beat his fist on the arm of his chair. "There is talk in Court of a marriage between the Duke of Norfolk and Mary Stuart. The Queen knows of it, though none can tell if she likes it or not. But such a marriage would mean we could pack the Stuart woman back to her Scottish kingdom with an English husband who might make her forget her love for the French. I favour such a match myself, for then Elizabeth could name Mary Stuart's son as heir to the

English throne. Mary's son James is being reared a Protestant, and he could ensure the Protestant succession for England."

He rose from his chair and paced the room like a restless cat.

" But what we have just learned from Master Weaver puts a different complexion on the matter. Norfolk wants not only the Scottish throne but the English one and all! It is more serious than most men think. Yorkshire, yes, and those defiant Earls who strut the Scottish Marches like fighting cocks are a long way from London. In London, men do not trouble about what is afoot north of the river Trent!"

Sir Ralph was a northerner. He knew how a northerner thought. On the surface all was calm, but the Catholic religion in the north lay like dregs at the bottom of a jug. Given but a little stir, they would rise to the top.

" Will you go to London and warn the Queen?" he asked.

" No, Ralph. I am President of the Council here in the north, and in York I must stay. The Queen would not take it kindly if I were to arrive in London without her permission, for however good a cause."

Sir Ralph was learning the ways of diplomacy. " Then will you play a waiting game?"

" I cannot do that either. The yeoman spoke of de Spes and Alva. How could a simple countryman know of these Spaniards, still less connect them with Mary Stuart? I think the matter has gone too far for delaying."

" Then what is to be done, my Lord?"

" I shall not disturb the Queen, Ralph. When she

E*

worries she becomes sick in her stomach. I will write to the Queen's Secretary—aye, and Walsingham also—that pure Protestant nose of his will smell out a plot if one is there."

He took up his quill.

" I will write letters alike—one to Cecil and one to Walsingham. In an hour I shall need two men to ride separately to London. Appoint these men Queen's Messengers, and give them all the privileges that these appointments warrant. Have we two such men of trust in this city of churches?"

" Aye, my lord. A thousand and two!"

" Then make haste, good friend."

The Earl of Sussex began to write.

FOURTEEN

THE FIRST fog of November rolled across the water-meadows, then slowly and silently wrapped Aldbridge in a soft damp blanket. Sir Crispin Wakeman shivered, pulling his bed-covers over his head, and thought of the stonemasons and plasterers and wood-carvers who would have to be paid now that the alterations to the Manor chimneys were finished. But he would receive his reward and more besides when the rightful Queen of England sat on her throne. Mary Stuart would be generous to those who had helped her. The news brought by Northumberland's messenger two weeks ago had not been good.

The Duke of Norfolk had let himself be thrown into the Tower. Now the Earl of Northumberland had received despatches smuggled from Norfolk's prison, urging the men in the North who supported Mary Stuart's cause to lie low.

Those Southerners were too tender—too easily deterred from their bounden duty. Tomorrow, decided Sir Crispin at the meeting at Topcliffe, he would urge most strongly that men who had no stomach for fighting should stay at home and sew with their womenfolk!

Sir Crispin closed his eyes, and prepared to dream of glories to come.

Anne stirred in her sleep then settled her head in the crook of her husband's arm.

" John?"

" Hush." Gently John Weaver stroked her cheek. " Go to sleep again. All is well."

All is well! All would be well if a man could forget that the garrisons in York and Knaresborough had been alerted. All would be well if a man were not suddenly suspicious of his neighbour—if whispers could be stilled. All would be well if Mary Stuart could be marched home across the Scottish border instead of being guarded at Tutbury like a queen bee in a hive. If the north country did not bubble and seethe like a witches' cauldron of plots and intrigues, all would be well.

" Sleep, Anne, for I shall not," thought John Weaver. " Sweet Jesus, will this Judas ever sleep contented again?"

Peter, the miller, lifted the loose stone in the hearth and pointed to the gold coins it concealed.

" These five sovereigns will be sufficient for your needs should I be long away and there is flour and salted meat that you may eat reasonably well. Guard your food, wife. Soon money will not buy it. The bad summer was a curse from Almighty God because men turned their backs on the true faith. But that will be soon be put to rights—what say you, lads?"

But unlike his brother, Jeffrey was silent. Holding his head high he faced his father, his hands clammy with the sweat of apprehension.

" Edward, my brother, may do as he pleases, but if

you fight for the Queen of Scotland, sir, you fight without me!"

Disbelieving, the miller cleared his throat.

" So! We have on our midst one of small faith and great cowardice it would seem!"

" No, sir. But if I am man enough to fight, then I am man enough to have a mind of my own. I will not take up arms in Mary Stuart's name. I have no stomach to die for a cause that brought the death of my betrothed, nor will I fight alongside one whom I would glady stick through if the chance were mine!"

In the candlelight of the warm mill kitchen, son faced father like the bitterest of enemies.

" I swear to you, sir, that if you force me to take up arms, the first man to die in this your cause, will be Kit Wakeman!"

Winifrede, the priest's wife, lay quiet in her bed. There was a silence about the night so ominous she could almost hear its whispered warning. Mischief was in the air. Lately men had been to confession who were known Catholics. Something was afoot when such men used the services of a married priest—something was amiss when men so feared for the state of their souls that almost daily now they unburdened their sins to her husband.

Nor could all Winifrede's nagging drag one word from the priest to satisfy her curiosity. Many years ago, when she had married the young monk nurtured in the ways of the old religion then turned out of his abbey by Henry Tudor, it seemed they had grasped the best of both worlds. But Mary Tudor's accession had soon put paid to double beds for priests, and Winifrede's husband had lost his living, for Mary Tudor's priests *must* be celibate!

Now, for many years, all had been well. Elizabeth did not like her clergy to be married, but those who were could usually procure a reasonable country parish. Winifrede Sedgwick did not wish to leave her comfortable house in Aldbridge and the good living they enjoyed—for a good living it was, if only from the shilling fines paid by dissenting Catholics. Now her husband was hearing Catholic confessions. Was he ready then to turn his coat again, and cast her aside? By God, she vowed, she would find out before morning what was afoot!

Before another winter came, if God spared her, Goody Trewitt decided she must buy another blanket for her bed. But blankets cost money and of that she had precious little. The only way she could find more warmth for her bed would be by way of the Parish Chest, and that Goody was too proud to do. The bad summer had caused food prices to rise. Before another harvest had been gathered, Goody's purse, she knew, would be as empty as her belly.

Sir Crispin had not been as generous of late as he might. This was the first winter he had forgotten the poor of the village. Men hereabouts seemed occupied with other things, of that Goody was sure.

A midwife who is called out in the small dark hours of the morning sees and hears much that is unusual—the rumbling of a cart, or a horse with muffled hooves making for the Manor; and Peter the miller's dying mother asking a blessing on Queen Mary who had been lodged up the dale in Castle Bolton.

More the pity the Scottish Queen was ever there at all,

thought Goody, with men flocking to her like flies round a honey jar! Mary Stuart was at the bottom of the unrest. God! What fools men were who could not let well alone. To even the score, Goody asked a blessing on Queen Elizabeth, and closed her eyes.

Those citizens of York who had a mind to, slept easy on Martinmas Eve, for the stout walls surrounding them were patrolled by the newly alerted militia. But safeguarding their homes and possessions was one thing—taking up arms for Elizabeth Tudor was another, and that Sir Ralph Sadler knew.

York was a city of churches where the old faith was taking long to die. Today, he was told, Sussex's spies had learned of a meeting at the Earl of Northumberland's estate in Topcliffe, scarcely a spit away, and to that meeting would go openly most of the Catholic nobles of the district.

The northern Earls had become a law unto themselves, setting Elizabeth's parliament at defiance without fear. What would happen if the militiamen of York were ordered to fight? Many would refuse. Many, once armed, might desert to Mary Stuart's cause. Sir Ralph Sadler was uneasy. The jug was being stirred. The dregs were rising . . .

Kit Wakeman threw logs on the fire. Outside in the foggy mist, nothing stirred. It was as though everything waited for the signal. Tomorrow, he would ride with his father to Topcliffe when once and for all time would be settled what was to be done. There had been too much delaying. Mary Stuart could have been taken from her prison long ago. Last Christmas she had still been held at

Castle Bolton. It would have been easy then. Kit thought back to that Christmas.

It had been good, for it was then he had first proved his manhood. Last Christmas he had got himself a bastard, and now Meg Weaver was dead. If only she had not called out to him that day of the beggars he would not be sitting here now, troubling about his conscience. Why had she been so stupid?

It had taken a lot of talking to convince his father that John Weaver would not betray the cause. His father had slapped him about the ears as though he were a child and an idiot.

"If you must lay a maid, get you to York. Don't take one on your own doorstep!" his father had stormed.

Kit had liked Meg. She had been small and fragile. She'd felt good in his arms, and he would remember her always. They said you always remembered the first one. For all her elfin frailness, there had been a fire in Meg that had matched his own. He had thought a lot about the night she had died. It was frightening to remember the trance from which she had whispered to him.

I will come again, Kit! One day, I will have you. Wherever you are, I will find you.

But she was dead, and she couldn't have him. He wondered where she was buried. Old Sedgwick had refused her the church. Where was she now? It didn't matter, really, but she had died unshriven and without absolution. Where was her soul now? Was it looking for *his* soul? Hastily Kit Wakeman crossed himself. Damn old Sedgwick! He had refused Meg the Last Rites, and now her soul was in Purgatory.

Soon the call to arms would come, and there had been no Catholic priest in the district for weeks. God only knew when another would arrive. Some men of the cause were confessing to old Sedgwick, so fearful were they for their immortal souls. Well, let them! Kit Wakeman would never unburden to an Anglican priest!

But he needed to make his confession. He wanted to go into battle clean and absolved; but how could he, when there was no priest to hear him? He wanted to free himself of the guilt he felt for Meg Weaver's death. He wanted to be rid of her tormented soul.

He must be his own confessor! St. Olave would help him, for she was his patron saint. He had been born on her day, and baptised in the church dedicated to her. St. Olave would intercede for him and bring absolution. He would write his confession and leave it in the newly-built secret place where the chalice and vestments for the travelling priest were kept. What more holy a place than that?

The chill fog lifted from the river, softening the mutilated stones of St. Mary's Abbey and penetrating the chinks and cracks of the walls of the King's Manor.

" Is there anywhere a place so cold as this city of York?"

The Earl of Sussex pulled his furs around him, reluctant to leave the warmth of the fire for the chill of his bed-chamber.

"I would believe the men who said this house was thrown up in three months," he grumbled into his goblet. " 'Tis damp, 'tis gloomy, and the four winds of heaven blow between every brick and stone."

Sussex had long ago expected to return to the London

Court. Now, it seemed, he would never see his home again. He had warned the Queen of the plot that was hatching more than two months ago.

"Watch," came back the reply. "Watch, and wait."

The Queen always said that. She knew how to watch and wait. She had learned the lesson well in her childhood. But watching and waiting in this dreary north was an insecure business. The spies were in, and their reports had long since been despatched to Sir Francis Walsingham. The known rebels had been named—Norton, Vavasour, Wakeman, Markenfield, Tempest the Stormcock and Tankard—most of the great families in the county. Now in part, the watching was over, for at last the Queen had decided to act.

The Earls of Westmorland and Northumberland were known to be in Topcliffe. At noon that day, Sussex had despatched a messenger from York. See how brave the Earls would be when they received the Queen's command to report to London. Before daybreak the messenger would be back, and with the answer he carried would come, for good or evil, an end to the watching and waiting.

In the room beneath the eaves of John Weaver's farmhouse, stupid Polly slept snug in her bed, a smile on her vacant face. By her side in the rocking cot, a tiny baby, passing two months old, lay snugly covered with lambskins, a dribble of Polly's milk still wet on his chin.

Only the innocent and the stupid slept soundly on that night of the first fog of November.

FIFTEEN

FROM THE turrets of Micklegate Bar the archers with bow-strings taut, followed the progress of the horseman as he rode towards them through the mist of early morning.

"Hold your fire!" The Captain of the Guard held up his hand. "He is a Queen's rider. Lift the portcullis!"

The archers let go their breath, and lowered their bows. Slowly the great spikes rose and the rider who wore the insignia of a Queen's Messenger, passed beneath the gate of the great grey fortress into the city of York, and on towards the King's Manor.

An urgent knocking awoke the Earl of Sussex. Stiffly he rose from his chair.

"What is it, Ralph?" he demanded peevishly.

"The messenger from Topcliffe, my Lord. He's back!"

Sussex blinked open his eyes and turned to meet the dishevelled rider who ran up the steps and into the hall. Without a word he handed back the unopened message he had been charged to deliver to the Earls of Westmorland and Northumberland.

"They were gone?"

"Aye, my Lord. Not sight nor sound of them. I rode

back by way of Ripon. The Minster bells there rang out almighty strange, my Lord—the peals rang backwards! And all along the way, though it was scarce light, I heard the ringing of church bells in every village I passed through."

Sir Ralph Sadler's eyes met those of Sussex. There was no need for words.

" You have done well, this night." Sussex addressed the man. " What is your name?"

" Thomas, my Lord Earl, from Pontefract."

" Leave us, Thomas, and hold your tongue. Say nothing of what you saw and heard this night. You will be rewarded."

With a bow, the messenger departed.

" So," Sussex threw down the sealed parchment. " The birds are flown and the tocsin rings out! It has come, Ralph. They are wily foxes, those border Earls. They knew or guessed they were to be ordered to London. Far from filling them with fear, the Queen's command has driven them to defiance. 'Tis fine for Her Grace to issue her orders from the safety of London town. 'Tis another thing to enforce them in this wilderness. Now she has called their bluff, and we have an uprising on our hands!"

When daylight came and the great wooden gates of the Bars of the city walls were left unopened and portcullises were not raised, the citizens of York scented danger. Those who lived outside the walls picked up what they could carry and driving their livestock before them, demanded entry into the safety of the fortress city.

The clanging of the bell of St. Olave's church awoke

the village of Aldbridge. Some were mystified and wondered what its urgent clamour could mean, but those who understood, ran with thudding hearts to the Green, then on to the Manor, for their orders.

" The day has come," called Sir Crispin Wakeman, " when Englishmen rise up and fight for the true faith, aye, and for the true Queen!"

" The true faith!" went up the shout.

" Mary for our Queen!"

" Come now, and arm yourselves!" Sir Crispin held high his sword. " And let us to Ripon. God is on the side of the righteous! In God's name we fight!"

Zealously the men of Aldbridge formed themselves into a column behind Sir Crispin and his retainers.

" God is for us!" they cried, and headed towards the church.

On the wall of the bell-tower of St. Olave's hung the levy arms—pikes and bows and quivers of arrows kept in safety in the church until such times as England might demand her levy of men from the village to fight in her defence. Some men carried their own bows or lances. Others took what arms were kept within the church. Some lifted the great fire-hooks that lay in the church porch and brandished them on high.

From beneath the altar where they had lain for thirty years, men took out the hidden banners and the silver crucifix of the Pilgrimage of Grace. Half a lifetime ago, men in Yorkshire had risen in peaceful petition, asking Queen Elizabeth's father to restore England to the Church of Rome, and begging the removal of heretic Anglican priests. Their banners had borne the Five Wounds of

Christ. Their protests had been mild and their cause, they believed, was just.

Henry Tudor's revenge had been bloody and terrible, yet now it seemed it had been forgotten. Encouraged by many who should have known better, fostered by old hatreds and urged on by the scheming of Spain, the men of the northern counties were marching once again.

Sir Crispin Wakeman held high the banner.

" See these Wounds of Christ? See this banner, long hidden beneath an altar sacriligiously used? Our fathers died for their beliefs, and now we shall do likewise, if God wills. This time, our cause shall triumph!"

Thus armed and encouraged, a score good men made for the house of the priest.

" 'Tis the rabble," hissed Winifrede. " They have taken the levy arms from the church and now demand a blessing to take them on their way. Be gone by the side door, for you'll not give succour to those damned Papists!"

Father Sedgwick wriggled uneasily. He was torn by uncertainty, and now he must choose. If the Stuart cause triumphed and he had refused his blessing, he would have to answer to Sir Crispin. But priests who openly acknowledged Queen Elizabeth's enemies might well have cause to regret it!

" What am I to do, wife?" His pale hands shook. " Either way I am lost."

" I'll tell you what's to be done! You'll away to the house of the fox-catcher, and give succour to his old mother!"

" But his mother is not dying, and Barnabas lives all of two miles down river," protested the priest.

" Good, and better for my liking if it were three miles!
It is time you visited your outlying parishoners. By God's
Holy Mother, husband, you'll have me to answer to if you
bless this gathering. If you are not here, then none can
blame you for what you might do, or what you refuse
to do!"

Flinging her husband's cloak in his face, Mistress
Sedgwick pushed him through the back door.

" We want no renegade priest to bless us!" yelled the
men of Mary Stuart's cause when the priest's wife told
them her husband was tending the sick, two miles away.
" Let's to Ripon and the Minster! There we can have a
blessing from a true man of God!"

" Devil take the lot of you," muttered Winifrede as she
slammed and bolted the door, " and God save Elizabeth,
our Queen!"

A fresh breeze smacked down from the hills and blew
away the fog that had shrouded the night, and seizing the
Banners of Grace that had long lain dark and airless, it
tossed them on high, snapping at their corners and streak-
ing out their pennants as they were held aloft by the men
of Mary Stuart's cause.

" So this is what has been brewing." Goody Trewitt
watched the men of Aldbridge as they straggled past John
Weaver's farm. " This is why men have walked on egg-
shells of late, and nerves have twanged like bowstrings."

She turned to Anne and John who stood beside her.

" Did you know of this, John Weaver?"

" Aye, I knew of it. I knew only too well!"

" So!" Anne's eyes met John's. " This is why my husband has tossed and muttered in his sleep these two

months gone. This is what took him to York to seek out
Walter Skelton. You heard more that night at the Manor
than you told me of!"

"Aye, Anne, I heard more—much more."

John Weaver looked away from the searching eyes.

"And that night when you journeyed to York? You did
not see Walter Skelton."

John shook his head. "No. Walter was in Lincoln. I
saw the Earl of Sussex."

"I understand," whispered Anne. "Now it all makes
sense to me."

"Forgive me, dearest Anne. I was overcome with grief,
and Meg's death weighed heavily upon me. I was bitter
and wanted revenge . . ."

"God, see how they go, the knaves and jackanapes!"
Goody Trewitt spat upon the ground. "Anne Weaver, I
could find it in my heart to forgive a man who had betrayed
that rabble. Could you not, also?"

Anne reached for John's hand and held it tight.

"They march with the Banners of Grace for a talisman.
They will fight in God's name and die, maybe, for what
they believe to be right. With all my heart I hope they
perish as Meg perished and lie unshriven as she lies!
Damn them, and damn the woman they fight for. May
they all rot in hell!"

Viciously she spat as though to rid her mouth of the
curse she had uttered, then covering her face with her
hands she turned to John's arms.

"Forgive you? Dear love, there is nothing to forgive.
Had you but told me what you had done, I could have
given you comfort. Come." She held out her hand to

Goody. "Forget them, and let us break our fast."

Singing and chanting, the latter-day Pilgrims carried their banners and crucifix through the village, and made for the crossroads. At their head rode Sir Crispin, with Kit for his squire. Behind them jogged Peter the miller on the great horse that pulled his corn wagon, his eldest son walking tall by his side. The spirits of the band of men were high as their banners as they marched, calling to men who watched to join them for God and the cause of Mary Stuart.

At the crossroads by the stone-pit they paused, then set their sights for Ripon to join with others of their faith who would now be assembled there. And Kit Wakeman rode proud, his soul confessed and cleansed, sword by his side, holding aloft the pennant that bore Christ's Wounds. He was a man, and would fight and die like one if needs be.

He did not notice the pathetic scattering of rubble as he passed the stone-pit. Above his head, a lone plover hovered on the breeze.

" Pee-wit-wit-wit," it piped sadly, but Kit did not hear its hopeless call.

SIXTEEN

MEN WHISPERED in the inn at Aldbridge that there had been close on four thousand foot-soldiers and two thousand riders and horses camped on Bramham Moor. They had marched in from Ripon and Richmond and Tadcaster, calling for men of the Catholic faith to join them; overthrowing communion tables and stamping the English prayer books underfoot in churches along their route.

The Earl of Sussex held York for Queen Elizabeth, but the great gates of the city were closed fast so that no one could enter and none slip out to join the rebels. Some of Northumberland's army had marched south, making for Tutbury and Mary Stuart, but she had been snatched away yet again and taken to Coventry Castle out of reach of her rescuers.

And Englishmen had not risen to join the cause as the rebels had hoped, and in village after village as they marched south the men they expected to flock to their banners had turned away in sullen silence. Retaliation had been speedy and terrible and the Queen of England killed for all time the sneer of Mary her half-sister, and proved herself to have been fathered by a Tudor.

Three armies of well-trained and trusted men took to the field for Elizabeth and routed the rebellious northmen, for pikes and pasternosters were no match for the armour and guns of the Queen's men. The glorious uprising for which so many had plotted and prayed became an ignominious defeat.

The southern armies surged on through the cold and hungry counties of the north, taking all they could plunder and burning and ravaging the already impoverished country-side. Christmas came and went that year with little mention and no rejoicing.

Whipped by the east wind, with clothing tattered and feet bare and bleeding, the starving remnants of the rebel army slunk over the Border like flea-riddled dogs to the shelter of Scottish sympathisers. The uprising was dead. Elizabeth Tudor's church was safe. The Queen's Majesty was inviolate.

And after the subjugation of the north came retribution, for the Queen's tolerance was played out. She had been lenient, allowing for private worship and turning a blind eye to it. She had never, she declared, wished to look into a man's conscience. She had loved all her people, Anglican and Catholic and Protestant as though they were her children, and they had turned against her like spoiled and wilful brats!

The royal temper rose to a fury as Elizabeth paced the floor of her castle at Windsor.

" I demand you make an example of these people and make it greatest in the towns of Ripon and Tadcaster," she ranted. " And if you do not find sufficient rebellious dogs in those towns, go out into the hamlets and villages

around. Crush them, I say, crush them! I will be monarch
in my own realm!"

Then she clutched her stomach for the nervous pains
she felt in times of stress were too much for her to bear.
The great and glorious Elizabeth Tudor vomited for all
around her to see.

The rebels straggled home, hungry and afraid, looking
over their shoulders for the finger of revenge that soon
would point at their misdeeds. And men barred their
doors against them in the village of Aldbridge and turned
their backs and refused them food, for no one dared
succour the enemies of the Queen.

In Ripon and Tadcaster, men under suspicion were
dragged from their homes and taken in chains to York for
questioning and there they met Master Topcliffe, Catholic-
hater and torturer extraordinary; met too his barbaric
collection of tongue-looseners. Those who were known to
Walsingham's spies were put to death and for most, death
was kinder than life during that hellish winter in the
county of York.

From Aldbridge was demanded payment of two souls
for the treachery of the village and the Queen's avengers
battered on the doors of the manor house to claim their
due. But the manor had long stood silent and deserted.
Sir Crispin and Kit Wakeman had not returned to their
home, and Lady Hilda had ridden out under cover of
darkness on St. Stephen's Eve, and none knew or cared
where she had gone.

Ravening like wolves and howling for their prey, the
blood-crazed soldiers had vented their disappointment on
the mill, wrecking the heavy granite millstones and making

a bonfire of the miller's furniture to warm their freezing fingers and toes. Then they had taken Peter and his eldest son and whipped them through the village to the gaunt black elm on Gibbet Hill, and left the roughly hanged bodies to swing in the biting wind as a warning to all of the absolute mortality of man.

And whilst the frost-blackened corpses danced a death jig over the unyielding February earth, John Weaver sat by his fire and thought back to the time he had last known contentment. Would a man might recognise happiness for what it is at the moment in time in which it happens. Then he could know to hold it precious and golden in his heart to remember for all time.

One of those rare moments he knew now, had been the soft warm night in midsummer when the blackbird on the apple tree had piped an evening hymn; when the smell of new-cut hay had filled the air and Meg had run laughing down the path to welcome Walter Skelton and his shabby little donkey.

Anne held out her hand. " What are you thinking of, John?"

" I was thinking of happier days, but it is wrong of me. There are some not so fortunate as we. I heard today that the Earl of Northumberland was taken from his prison at Lochleven and brought to York for execution. They say his head is stuck on a pole over the Bar at Micklegate."

" Do you have pity for such a man?" Anne turned to her husband, disbelief in her eyes. " Were it not for him and his like we would not sit here now, our bellies rumbling with hunger and fearing for our lives! Had not Mary Stuart desired to rule England we would not be treated as cattle by the soldiers who strut about the place. Men have paid who had no part in the uprising. But the innocent will always suffer with the guilty."

John piled logs into the grate. Empty bellies did not ache so much in the warmth of a fire. Anne was right. The first of the innocents had been Meg. Sweet fair Meg, whose sad little ghost was always by his side.

" John, dear heart," Anne knelt before him and took his hands in hers, " forgive me if I grumble. We have much to be glad about. We have the babe for comfort in our old age, and soon spring will be here and we will sow our crops and reap our harvest once again. And there is Goody." She smiled with affection at the old midwife who snored by the fire. " Let us waken her. I have bone broth in the stock-pot and there is a little bread. And we have each other, John. What else matters?"

It seemed to Anne that the Fates listened in her chimney, ever ready to make a mockery of her words. The banging on the door sent a shiver down John's spine and awoke the old woman who slept in the ingle. Slowly John rose to his feet, reluctant to open the door.

" God help us!" cried the terrified Goody. " They have come to take us!"

Anne remained on her knees, her eyes staring at the door. In the cot, Meg's baby stirred and cried in his sleep, and Polly cowered in the corner and held tight to Goody's trembling hand. John walked to the door and drew back the bolt.

A trooper stood on the doorstep.

" Is this the house of John Weaver?" he asked.

John looked at the tall broad-shouldered soldier, his

mouth dry, the bitter wind biting at his burning cheeks.

"I am John Weaver," he replied gravely, "and this is my house."

"Well met, sir." The man held out his hand. "I am Martin Hewitt of Lord Clinton's regiment, in the service of Queen Elizabeth. My orders are to escort you to York."

"To York?" Anne gasped out the words. "What is amiss that you must take my husband to York?"

"I have not come to *take* your man, mistress. I am charged to escort him there. I am not arresting Master Weaver, just asking that he come with me to York, to the lodgings of the Earl of Sussex."

John stood still, his hand on the door latch. The searching wind scattered the wood-ash in the fireplace and sent puffs of smoke curling to the ceiling.

"Will you step inside, Master Hewitt? The wind blows too cold this night for standing on door-stones."

"That I will, sir, and right gladly." Martin Hewitt rubbed his hands together. "It is a long cold ride from York. I have horses tethered by the gate. Would there be shelter for the poor beasts? They have ridden hard and stand there sweating."

John took a birch twig and carefully lit his lantern.

"Come," he said, "and I will light you to the stable."

Anne rose from the hearth where she had remained since the knocking on the door had frozen her into immobility and softly closed the door behind the two men.

"He seems to be a kind man," she whispered, "for he worries about his horses."

"Aye," agreed the old woman, her knees still trembling beneath her petticoats. "His face seems honest enough.

But mind what you say, Anne, or he may carry off the cow and the heifer without a by-your-leave. They're all the same, these southern soldiers with their looting and raping."

From the corner where she crouched with the baby, Polly whimpered. Anne held out her hand.

" Come to bed, Polly. Pull the blankets over your head and the soldier will not see you." Gently she led the trembling girl to the staircase. " It is warm and safe in bed, and I will bring you up a posset later. Master Weaver will not let the man harm you."

Long before daylight, John Weaver folded a blanket round his belongings and tied the bundle with leather thongings.

" Before many weeks have passed I shall be back, Anne. Send for Jeffrey if you are in need. He is a good lad and will help you. Goody will stay with you whilst I am gone. Remember, love, do not open the door to anyone after nightfall."

Over the supper table she had talked to Martin Hewitt as they drank their broth and ate their meagre slice of bread. He had told her of the wonders of London town; of the actors who graced the stages on the South Bank, and the elegant houses on the sandy strand by the Thames and fashionable women who lived in them. Eyes glowing, he had repeated passed-on tales from Elizabeth's Court and told of the great ships that sailed into the very heart of the city, then sailed out again to all corners of the wide world, trading wool for spices and silks, or searching for the slow-moving treasure ships of the Spaniards.

His eyes had softened as he spoke of Mary, Bess and

Edward his children, named for three children of King Harry-God-rest-him. He had explained that he was a levy-man from the village of Southwark, across the river from London, called to the Queen's service to fight the northern rebels, and that soon he would go home to his last, for when he was not soldiering he made boots.

The jolly talkative man had broken down Anne's instinctive distrust for a while, but now it was time for the two men to leave, and she was afraid once more.

" John, dear heart, I will not see you again! " she sobbed. " Sweet Jesus, what have we done that was so wicked?"

But Anne knew what they had done; they had been too happy. The Fates are jealous of those who are too happy.

" No, Anne, do not cry." John held the tear-stained face in his hands. " I will come back. Trooper Hewitt is to escort me to York. Time is short, for tomorrow the Earl of Sussex rides to London, and I am to travel with the soldiers who ride with him. I will be in good and safe company. The Earl is close to the Queen. Nothing will harm me on the journey."

" I do not believe what he says."

Anne glanced defiantly at the trooper whose great bulk overshadowed even John's broad back.

" 'Tis true, mistress. I was instructed by Sir Ralph Sadler to request Master Weaver's company, and tell him to make preparations to travel to London. He will not be thrown into prison, mistress."

" All the same, sobbed Anne, " I shall never see his face again."

Martin Hewitt laid a kindly arm around the drooping shoulders.

F

" I promise you, ma'am, your good man shall be my personal charge. I will bring him back to you safe and sound. On the lives of my sweet children, I promise it."

" But why must he go to *London*?" Desperately Anne tried to delay the moment of parting.

" I do not know, for sure. Perhaps to see our Queen." The soldier grinned and winked at John. " Wish us God-speed, mistress."

" God go with you," whispered Anne.

She stood in the doorway until horses and riders were swallowed up by the darkness and their hoof-beats could no longer be heard. Dejectedly she turned back into the kitchen, quietly closing and barring the door.

" Stay with me, Goody," she whispered, " for I have never been so alone in my life."

SEVENTEEN

SADDLE-SORE and weary, John Weaver reined in his horse and stiffly dismounted, his eyes following the direction of Martin Hewitt's pointing finger.

" Look! There is it! There lies London before you. The most beautiful city in the world awakens and lights its fires. We are safe and sound, good John. We are home!"

It seemed to John that the whole world must be kindling its fires, for the woodsmoke that mingled with the thick black smoke of the newly fashionable sea-coal to form a drifting grey pall over the rooftops of London was one of the strangest sights John had ever witnessed.

" As we draw nearer, you will be able to pick out the river and the tall spires of the churches. Before long we shall ride through yonder streets below us and men will stop their work and run to watch us as we pass. And when we have safely delivered my Lord Sussex to Westminster, we will away to my home, and there you shall stay until the Queen makes known her wishes."

" I think, Martin, I shall always remember this morning," laughed John as he rubbed his aching body, " if only because at last my backside and this mare can part company."

Their journey had been tedious and slow, for the poor roads were made practically impassable by the bad weather. When horses and carts and the litters of the Queen's servants were not slipping and sliding on icy tracks, they stuck in water-filled pot-holes, when sometimes the wind blew warmer from the south and melted the frost-hard earth.

Most nights they had broken their journey at one of the great houses along their route, and John had been billeted with the troopers in stables or servants' quarters, and had slept warm and eaten well. In the dark nights as he lay beneath yet another strange roof, John's empty arms had longed for Anne.

As he belched contentedly from a stomach full of food, miraculously conjured from thin air for the Queen's servants and soldiers, John wondered guiltily if Anne had eaten that night as well as he had eaten, and knew without a shadow of a doubt that she had not. John knew too that Anne's thoughts would be for him; knew that she would fear for his safety and pray each night for his safe return.

He had learned no more about the purpose of his summons to London, for Sir Ralph Sadler had not been able to help him, and the Earl of Sussex had no time to spare for John's worries. Martin had made light of John's fears.

" Depend on it, good John, your visit is a result of a whim of the Queen, though why she should single you out for her favours I'll swear I do not know. Have you met the Queen?"

" I have not," John said, and scuffed the ground with his toe, like an anxious schoolboy.

" Have you done the Queen a service, then?"

" No, Martin, nor that either, though I weave a fair length of cloth. Who knows? Perhaps it is the services of a good Yorkshire weaver her Majesty needs?"

But John was still not sure why he had been called to Court, and every day that took him nearer to the capital saw him grow a little more anxious, and a little less sure that he would ever return to Anne and the baby again.

Now they were within sight and sound of the greatest city in Christendom. Soon, for good or ill, John would know why he had been summoned to the presence of Elizabeth Tudor.

Like all cities, London had its stinking gutters and rat-infested streets. Only outside the city walls, where noblemen and rich merchants had built their fine houses along the banks of the river, could the choking stench of close-packed humanity be left behind.

Although John found London to be much like York, but bigger, dirtier and noisier, the people of London had a happy air about them, far different from the dour and sober citizens of York. There was food in plenty in London, and men were able to obtain good work and money to pay for it, aye, and for entertainments that would be considered frivolous and a waste of hard-earned money in the North.

The citizens of London, John had learned from Martin, went regularly to the Bear Pit at the Paris Gardens in Southwark village, and placed wagers on cock-fights and cheered on the hungry dogs that baited tethered bulls or blinded bears. At Shoreditch too, the " Theatre " Playhouse and the " Curtain " regularly presented one or another of Mr. Burbage's plays at prices most ordinary folk could afford to pay, and as John and Martin walked along the beautiful Strand, or dawdled in Cheapside or read the creaking signs of the shops around St. Paul's, John became more and more bemused with the bustle and brashness of it all.

" And there," pointed Martin, " is the finest shop in the world. Do you know that within that Royal Exchange, good John, a man may buy anything from a bun to a bonnet, or a whistle to a wench. I'll warn you though, that wenches hereabouts are costly to buy."

" To *buy*, Martin?" John could not understand that women could be bought like sheep. " Can a man buy a woman in the city of London?"

Martin slapped his thigh and roared out his amusement.

" Nay, John, I'll swear you are callow as an unbloodied youth! You buy the use of their bodies for an hour or a night, as your purse warrants. Surely you know of these women?"

But John who had never travelled farther than the market at Richmond or the great grey walls of York had only seen tavern wenches who would bed with a man for the price of a tankard of ale. Nor was he interested in such doxies, for the love of his wife was generous and satisfying to him, and it was all he had ever known or wanted.

" I have heard of them, Martin," he replied, reluctantly interrupting his thoughts of Anne, " but I have never taken such a woman."

" Then be warned, friend. Take my advice and do not touch them—not even with a yardstick. They are shameless, John. They approach a man with their cheeks painted unnatural red, and their breasts all but popping out of their bodices. Turn away if one of them should wink an eye at you, for they bed with sailors who sail in from foreign parts, and take the pox from them. And God help a man who catches the pox, John. God help him. But a fig for that, for soon you will see the dearest sight on all the face of this earth."

They made their way through streets and alleys towards Billingsgate's port.

" It is a sight I would travel from the edge of the world to see," he enthused as they entered the yard of St. Magnus' church. " It is one of the wonders of the world, John!"

There before them was the panorama that was London's great bridge, built proud and broad across the wide river, with houses and shops that seemed to cling to its sides with invisible fingers, and hang suspended over the waters below.

" Come, John," urged Martin as they made for a gap between the close-packed houses from where they could look upriver, " can you see the fine houses of the merchants and nobles? And on the horizon is the Abbey of West-minster. Can your eyes pick it out? It is near the Abbey that our Queen holds her Court!"

John's eyes could easily see the squat outline of the great church, and nearer the palaces of earls and noble-men with their shining glass windows and gardens that swept down to the Thames.

" Ho! See them. Look, John, the apprentices!"

Martin pointed upstream to where a cluster of tiny boats filled with blue-smocked apprentices bobbed and bucked on the river as the tide turned and chopped back towards the sea.

"What are they about?" asked John anxiously, for the tiny boats seemed frail craft to sail such turbulent waters. "They are being drawn towards the great stone arches, Martin. They will surely be killed!"

But Martin laughed at his fears, and told him of the daring of the lads who "shot the arches" for the sheer devilment of it, steering their boats between the massive foundation piers as the rushing water hurtled beneath the gigantic arches like some enormous mill race.

As they watched, the tiny boats and the cheering devil-may-care apprentices were tossed safely out on the other side of the bridge and watchers threw coins into the boats, and pretty young girls threw kisses at the daring adventurers.

"Thank God," said John, heaving up a sigh of relief. "The young jackanapes are safe. Did you ever do such a foolhardy thing in your youth?"

"That I did," roared Martin with delight, "and had my ears boxed soundly for it by my father, God rest him. It's a part of growing up, like stealing apples and teasing girls."

They left the open side of the bridge and headed once again for the houses and shops and the shelter they gave from the cold downriver wind.

"Do you know, John, I have even seen *whales* from this bridge. I remember it fine, though it is more than twenty years ago, and before my soldiering days. I was a new apprentice and my master allowed us out to see the sight. Two great creatures they were that had swum into the

estuary, and men in boats killed them at Woolwich, then
pulled them upriver for the poor sickly young King to see.
I'll wager the sight of them must have frightened the lad
half to his death!"

John said nothing, but held his breath and braced his
body against the pushing crowds, resisting the cries and
entreaties of the shopkeepers as they offered their wares for
sale.

"Nay, friend," cautioned Martin as John fumbled in
his purse for a coin for a blind beggar, "keep your hand
on your penny. Yonder beggar is richer than the Lord
Mayor, I shouldn't wonder, and has eyes as keen as any
hawk's. I'll swear, John Weaver, you are so trusting you
need a keeper, or you'll come to harm in this city."

But just the same, John threw the coin to the beggar
and then laid his arm on Martin's shoulder and entered
into the fun of the afternoon. It was a long time, he thought,
as he jostled with the happy crowds that crossed the
bridge, since he had been so light-hearted. Perhaps the
black dog of remorse that sat so firmly on his shoulder was
tiring of his company. Maybe the good God was answering
his prayers at last, and giving him once again a quiet conscience and a peaceful mind.

"That's old Will Bridger's place," Martin jerked his
thumb over his shoulder as they passed a tiny shop set
precariously on the utmost edge of the bridge. "Do you
know it was once a chapel, dedicated to St. Thomas
Becket? It seems that the old King had a grievance against
the good saint, and issued him with a summons to
answer charges of rebellion against King Henry the
Second. Mind you, good St. Thomas didn't answer on

F*

account he'd been dead over three hundred years. So our Queen's good father made no more to-do, but turned the chapel into a grocer's shop. He was a sly old fox was Henry Tudor. He knew how to dispose of unwanted saints!"

"In faith, Martin," laughed John as they let the milling crowd push them along, "I think this London air has made me light-headed, for I feel free as a bird again!"

Martin grinned with pleasure that his sober Yorkshire friend had succumbed to the delights of his beloved city.

"There's a few up there," Martin pointed to the row of poles sticking above the gate of the drawbridge house in the centre of the bridge, "that would give a great deal to be as poor and happy as we two. There they rot, the Queen's enemies! That's where rebellious traitors end up, Good John. And it's all they deserve!"

Impaled on high was a row of several heads, gruesome beyond belief, a warning to all that treachery towards the Queen's majesty was a game played only by fools.

"I mind these younglings well," said Martin. "See them? The fair head and the red head, next to the long black-bearded one?"

"Maybe you'll know of these young blades. I was part of the escort that brought them from Ripon to London for execution. Norton, one was called. Christopher Norton, from Norton Conyers, not many miles from your home, John. Scarce a man—the youngest of seven sons, so I was told. Do you know the Nortons, John? Who the red-headed lad was who died with him, I forget, but he was noble-born and had a hand in the rebellion too. They were afraid, the pair of them, though they tried hard to be brave. I found it in my heart to pity them, though pity should not be given to the Queen's enemies."

John remained silent. It was best he did not speak, for he knew beyond all doubt the identity of the unknown boy of noble birth. He was glad at least that Martin had pitied him. That unknown boy had sat beside young Norton in Sir Crispin's kitchen and they had raised their glasses to *Marie*. Now the biting frosts and winds that whipped upriver had taken their toll of the youthful heads. The flesh was festered and black, and the boyish hair was matted with spray from the river below.

But there was no mistaking Kit Wakeman's curls. A man couldn't forget that flaming head of hair. John was glad the carrions had picked clean the eye sockets. It would have been hard to look into the dead eyes of those he had betrayed.

" He fathered a fine son," whispered John, nodding towards the stinking head that had once lain beside Meg's, " and he never owned him."

Martin looked at the stricken face of the man beside him.

" What did you say, John? I cannot hear above the din of this rabble."

" Nay, Martin," John shook his head, " it is of no importance. Come." He inclined his head to the opposite bank of the river. " This day has been too much for me. I weary for rest."

Pushing their way through the crowd, they walked down the roadway of the bridge and past the *Bear Tavern* to Southwark, where Martin's wife waited.

" Perhaps when you are rested good friend, we shall walk in the gardens and take the family to the bear-bating.

I tell you, John, there are such sights to be seen in this city, and such pleasures!"

But John Weaver's delight and wonder had been short-lived. A man does not like his conscience to stare at him from a maggot-riddled face. John only wanted to go home to Anne, and the comfort of her arms.

EIGHTEEN

FOR TWO days John Weaver and Martin Hewitt attended the Queen's court at Westminster, and for two days they waited in the anteroom or paced the corridor outside it, starting eagerly as the great doors of the audience chamber were thrown open, and another name called.

At first the bustle of the Court had fascinated John. Now his belly was rumbling, and it seemed they would be told to go home yet again and return on the following day.

" Never fret," said Martin, who seemed to know everything there was to know about life at Queen Elizabeth's court, and every person of importance who went in and out of the great doors, " we can wait here for many days before Her Grace has time to see you. There are many weighty matters she must deal with, and after all, she is but a woman!"

The great doors opened yet again and a man bowed himself out of the presence of the Queen. Her bodyguards closed the doors and slammed down their halberds as they stood to attention once more.

John looked at the great ash staves and the viciously sharpened battle-axes atop them. Lord, they would make short work of any who tried to pass them, he thought. What would happen, John wondered, if the man brought that heavy stave to attention on his toe instead of the floor? Would he bawl out loud with pain, or dance a jig, his sore foot in his hand? John could not imagine any such happening taking place, but what a change it would make from the everlasting waiting.

Martin's elbow dug urgently into John's ribs.

"They call your name, John. Remember to bow as the equerry told you!"

Martin gave him a shove and John was mighty grateful, for suddenly his feet had turned to blocks of stone. Slowly he walked towards the doors, his eyes on the red-uniformed pensioners and the weapons in their hands. Would they spring to attention as he walked through the doors? Would one of them slam *his* toe? The thought of it so intrigued him that he did not see the splendour of the great room, nor the courtiers, nor tall windows that sparkled pools of light on exquisite tapestries and jewel-sewn gowns. It seemed only that he walked endlessly until a restraining hand touched his arm.

John raised his eyes from the polished wood of the floor and looked at the Queen of England. It was as though he had come out of a dark place and gazed suddenly into the sun. He did not hear the rustle of satin and taffeta nor the murmurs of surprise and curiosity. He forgot all he had been told about bowing low. He stood quite still, his cap clenched in nervous hands, his eyes wet with tears.

So this was Elizabeth, Old Harry's wench. How could they have called her a music teacher's bastard? Her high forehead, the proud set of her head and her piercing amber eyes fathered her beyond all doubt. Around her head like the red-gold of a harvest moon shone the hair of a Tudor.

In that brief moment of encounter he gave her his soul. The golden image blurred and shifted as John's tears fell unchecked. He was not the first man to weep at the sight of Elizabeth Tudor.

The tongue-tied yeoman did not amuse the Queen as he amused some of her attendants. The sniggering stopped as she smiled and motioned to him to come closer.

" So here is one who cares for our Northern Kingdom? Tell us your name."

" I am John Weaver, Majesty, a yeoman of Aldbridge in the county of York, may it please you."

" It pleases us, John Weaver."

She looked at the guileless face and the tear-stained cheeks. He gazed at her, she thought, with the dumb adoration of a puppy—a puppy that would be whipped helpless in half a day by some of the silvered tongues around her. This man had no false graces. She wondered what sudden fancy had prompted her to bring him to London. Was she weary for the sight of one man who wanted nothing from her? Perhaps though, even this man had his price?

" What do you ask of us, John Weaver?"

" Ask, Madam? I ask nothing, for I have done nothing."

" Let us be the judge of that." The man *must* want something. Must hope for *some* reward. " Why then did you journey from York?"

" Because you commanded me, Ma'am."

The clear blue eyes met those of the Queen and held them steadily in their gaze.

" God's Blood, John Weaver, I'll swear I do believe you."

She threw back her head and gave a shout of laughter. The faces about her smiled. Suddenly she was tired of fawning courtiers and foxing ambassadors; sick of suspicion and the treachery of her nobles. Of Norfolk, Northumberland and Westmorland and even of Leicester whom she loved. She slapped the palms of her hands on the arms of her chair.

" Attend us, Burghley." She rose abruptly to her feet. " And you also Master Weaver."

The throng about the Queen parted as though gigantic hands had swept them aside. Noblemen bowed and women of title curtsied as Elizabeth Tudor, Lord Burghley her principal secretary and John Weaver, yeoman of Aldbridge walked through their ranks.

The door of the anteroom closed and Elizabeth Tudor flounced into a chair.

" Kat! Kat Ashley! God's Wounds, Burghley, we are weary of yonder company. *Kat Ashley*, are you deaf?"

" Not deaf, nor yet a thousand miles away. Hush your shouting, and let me take off your shoes." Mistress Ashley, First Lady of the Queen's Bedchamber, deftly removed the green leather pumps. " Did I not tell you this very morning they would pinch before the day was over? Will you never listen to old Kat? Now, my pretty, close your eyes, and Kat shall bathe your forehead with rose-water."

For a time there was quiet in the little room and the firelight flickered as it did in a kitchen in Aldbridge, half a world away. And a woman with a soothing tongue bathed away the ache in a Queen's head, and placed a cloth over her closed eyes. It seemed to John that they were the same ordinary people as those who sat beside Anne's hearth and admired the new fire-oven.

" Master Weaver?"

" Aye, Majesty?"

" Master Weaver, shall we tell you what those popinjays out yonder do now? They sink into chairs the minute we are out of the room. They take the weight of their sins off their feet and they think *Thank God*! And know you, Master Weaver, that at the slightest rattle of the handle on yon door, they will jump to their feet and the smiles will be back on their faces as if by magic."

The Queen did not expect an answer and John had the good sense to offer none. She placed her fingertips to the cloth that covered her eyes and sighed. Her hands thought John with amazement, were like those on the alabaster statues in the Minster of York, so white and exquisite they could have been the work of a sculptor. He must tell Anne about the Queen's hands, if he could remember. But this was all part of a dream, he knew it. Soon he would awaken.

Elizabeth Tudor removed the bandage from her eyes and digging her elbows into the soft arms of her chair pushed herself into a sitting position. Mistress Ashley settled the royal feet afresh on their stool and straightened and smoothed the folds of the royal gown before taking up her position behind the Queen's chair. Lord Burghley shuffled his aching feet and wished that he too might take the weight of his sins from them.

" Now tell us, Master Weaver—" Elizabeth was a Queen again. "—what prompted you to go to the Earl of Sussex at York? Did you desire revenge or reward? Or was it for love of your Queen, and hatred of Rome?"

The question was unexpected and direct. For a moment, John Weaver was startled.

" Speak man, we are privy here. There are none to hear save ourselves."

" Then I think, Madam, at first it was thoughts of revenge. I was bitter against those whose plotting became known to my little wench, and was the cause of her death. If she had not known what she did, she might yet have been alive. She was accused of witchcraft by the one who got her with child. He accused her to safeguard the plot to take your Majesty's throne."

" We have heard of these things from Sussex. But what of the girl? Was she a witch? Was it proven against her?"

" Nay, Madam. There was never a devil's mark on her. Mistress Trewitt, who washed her body, will swear to that with her dying breath."

Elizabeth nodded. She knew how easily an innocent could be caught up in intrigue. Had not she herself been called adultress and traitress by those around her sister Mary? Had she not, a virgin, been accused of bearing Tom Seymour's child? Had not Anne Boleyn her mother, stood accused of getting herself a crown by her witchcraft? Elizabeth Tudor understood these things.

" So, Master Weaver, you thought on revenge?"

" Aye, Madam, until I remembered those who lived and worked about me. I found I could not betray them."

" Why then did you seek out Sussex?"

" Because I saw the fair city of York and remembered the days of my apprenticeship there. Because I was grateful for years of peace and the end of burnings and hangings. And I saw a beggar's child that was ugly and mad, and I remembered my own little Meg, lying unblessed."

" You are an honest man, John Weaver. Had you said you did it for me alone, I would not have believed you. There are not many of your kind. You are a man we could trust."

The feeling of awe left John. His Queen was also a woman, and a lonely one at that.

" You can trust me with your life, Madam, and there are many like me in the North who honour you."

" Aye, now that I have cracked the whip and hanged men. Would to God I had not needed to do so. Had they but prayed privily, I could have turned a deaf ear. Do you believe your Queen, John Weaver?"

" Aye Madam, I believe you."

Then, almost as though she were ashamed of her outburst, Elizabeth straightened her shoulders and lifted her head.

" Tell me of the little maid's babe. Did it live?"

" Aye, Madam. She was delivered of a son before she died. We kept her secret and none knew she was with child save a few we could trust. We have claimed the child as our own, though some look askance that one of my wife's years could bear a child."

" How old is your wife?"

" She was born on the same day as yourself, Majesty, almost to the hour, and named Anne for your mother."

" Then we do solemnly declare she *can* bear a child! God's Blood man, your Queen is not too old to give an heir to England! Have you named the boy yet?"

" The midwife christened him. We could not ask the priest to take the child of an accused witch to the font. We called him Harry."

The Queen smiled and turned to the woman who stood behind the chair.

" That is a good name is it not, Kat? The babe is named for my father."

The Queen signalled to her Secretary.

" The purse, Burghley."

The audience was over. Elizabeth was tired. She held out her hand to John Weaver.

" Master Weaver, we thank you for your loyalty and good wishes." Elizabeth offered the leather purse. " We are pleased there are such men as yourself in our Northern provinces. Remember always your Queen. Go home to your wife, and the child, Harry, whom we declare to be your son. Care for him well, and guard his inheritance."

" I will love him like a father, but guard his inheritance I cannot, Madam. He has no inheritance. He is a bastard."

" God's Wounds!"

The purse in the Queen's hand hurtled across the room and a hundred gold sovereigns scattered to the floor and rolled and spun in all directions. " Teeth of hell, will I never hear an end to that accursed word? Would I could rub it from the English language. Could I but grind it under my heel into the midden from whence it came!"

She kicked aside her skirts and walked shoeless to the window.

" Damn you Kat Ashley, that you stand there silent. Men never called *you* bastard!"

She turned to face them, the later afternoon sun behind

her. Katherine Ashley had witnessed the Tudor temper before. Doubtless she would see it again. There was nothing to be said.

Lord Burghley did not betray by so much as the flicker of an eyelid what he thought or felt.

John Weaver hurried towards the door and waited for some sign that he should leave. For a moment the Queen stood still, deep in thought. Then suddenly as it began, the storm was over.

"You may leave us, Master Weaver. Attend us to-morrow at noon."

John bowed and opened the door. In the large chamber the chatterings stopped. A pageboy jumped to attention and men turned swiftly to face the door. With a rustle of petticoats women rose to their feet and smoothed their ruffled skirts. All were smiling. John followed the young boy across the room, his head held high.

"What lands have we in Yorkshire, Burghley?" the Queen asked.

"Lands, Your Grace?"

"Aye man. Lands of traitors who have fled 'ere they could be brought to trial for rebellion."

By our Lady, thought Lord Burghley, there sits a true chip off the old Tudor block!

The traitors who had fled, had been allowed to. Had they not, and had they been caught and tried under martial law for their part in the uprising, their lands would have not been forfeit, not even if those men had been found guilty of treason and executed at Tyburn. They had virtu-ally traded their estates for their lives, and Elizabeth, with the parsimonious guile of her grandfather, had allowed them to do so, and been the richer for it. Only the poorer people had died in the vicious reprisals.

" Burghley! Do you sleep on your feet?"

" Nay Madam, I do but think. What part of Yorkshire would interest Your Grace? Around Ripon, perhaps?"

" Aye, Burghley. Around Ripon."

" There is the house at Topcliffe owned by the Earl of Northumberland, and the great house at Norton Conyers. There is also a very fair house and farm at Markenfield. All these estates are forfeit to the Crown, Madam."

" Nay, Burghley, I have buyers for those estates. Lord Ellesmere has already offered well for Norton Conyers. I had in mind an inheritance for the babe, Harry. Let us not lose our heads in wildness. The rebellion cost money and it must be paid for. I cannot afford to be as generous as I would wish!"

Lord Burghley's eyes met those of Katherine Ashley. *This one runs truest to Tudor form than anything that ever drew breath*, they said.

" There is the manor house and village of Aldbridge. That might be appropriate, Your Grace."

Elizabeth clapped her hands with delight. " Were they the lands of the cur who snivelled at the heels of Norton and Markenfield? Was it not the son who . . .?"

Burghley nodded his head. " Aye Madam, it was the son who got Master Weaver's daughter with child. Your Grace would choose wisely to give that estate to the child. It would be almost like Divine Justice, Madam."

" Divine Justice!" Elizabeth nudged her Secretary with her elbow and shouted with laughter. " Divine Justice. I like that! Kat, we will drink a cup of wine. We will drink to Divine Justice! Now, Burghley, hear us good. We will tell you what you must do, and do before tomorrow!"

The Queen was in a fair mood again. By God's Holy Mother she silently vowed, before another day was run, there would be one bastard less in her Kingdom!

"Kat Ashley!" she yelled. "Where is our wine?"

NINETEEN

ANNE DID not recognise the trooper whose knocking roused her from bed in the cold half-light of the late March dawn.

" Bid you good morning, my lady."

Anne blinked her eyes open.

" Might I come in, my lady, and set down Sir John's packages?"

" Sir John?" repeated Anne, still only half awake.

" Aye my lady. Sir John—*your* husband," Martin Hewitt teased. " See?" He pointed to where John tethered the horses by the rowan tree. " I have brought him back safely to you as I promised."

" John, my love, you are back!" Arms outstretched, Anne ran to her husband. " God be praised, you are safe!"

She had not expected to see him again. She had lived from day to day, waiting for the awful news she was sure must come. But he was home and holding her close. He was safe again and her fears had been for nothing. She lifted her tear-filled eyes and looked again at his beloved face. As if to convince herself she were not still sleeping she touched it gently with her fingertips.

" John, you are so dear to me," were the only words she could find to tell him that her heart was about to burst with happiness.

Hands clasped like young lovers afraid to let each other go, they walked towards the farmhouse.

" I thought I was imagining it all." Anne was laughing now through her tears. " He called me ' me lady ' and you ' Sir John ' and I knew for sure I was dreaming. But you are here, John. You are back home."

She squeezed his hand tightly for reassurance, and John kissed the tears that lay on her cheeks and smoothed the hair that fell unplaited across her face.

" Yes, my Anne, I am home." He reached for the cloak that hung beside the door and gently wrapped it round her shoulders. " Now, my Lady Weaver, if you will make us some food, my good friend Martin and I will be forever in your debt."

" John!" admonished Anne. " The teasing must stop. You may leave your fine titles in London town. You are in Anne Weaver's house-place and not the palace of a Queen."

She turned from the fire she was kindling, the bellows in her hand.

" Did you see the Queen, John? I could not bear it had you not seen her."

" Yes Anne, I saw the Queen, and I have such to tell you whilst we eat, though I have seen such things we could eat a thousand breakfasts before I had told you all."

, Anne set plates of bread and bacon on the table.

" Let me pull off your boots, John, and we will take

our food before the little one awakes, and screams for Polly's breast."

" Is he well?" John was anxious for news of his newly-given son. " Does he thrive?"

" He is well and lusty, though it has been a bitter struggle to keep up Polly's food that he might become so. Thank God for a gentle spring. Jeffrey has sown the remainder of the wheat and rye." Tears that were still near the surface sprung again to her eyes. " Jeffrey has been like a son to me whilst you have been away. Would that he and Meg had married."

" Nay, sweet Anne, your husband forbids it. No more tears. Jeffrey shall have his reward. He shall have back his father's mill."

" I am glad." Anne wiped away her tears for the second time that morning. " But how do you know this?"

" Because it is mine, now, to give."

" John, what has gotten into your mind?" Anne shook her head in bewilderment. " Why is the mill yours to give?"

" Because this title says it is so. Because the Queen gave to me the stewardship and lands of Aldbridge. They are mine to hold in trust for Meg's babe. His father did not own him, but the Queen in her wisdom has set it to rights." Carefully he opened the deed and laid it on the table. " See, Anne, there is her name—Elizabeth—and her royal seal."

" You must not tease, John. I am not so learned as you." Anne would not be convinced. " You know I cannot read what is written there."

" 'Tis true my lady," Martin pointed to the words.

"See, there is your husband's name, *John Weaver*." Slowly he picked out the words, '. . . *and thence to the child Harry and to his heirs* . . .' Believe me, it is true. You are indeed the wife of a man of title."

Ann heard the words as though they had been shouted into some vast room and were echoing and re-echoing above her head. If what they told her were true, then Meg's baby would inherit the lands that one day would have belonged to Kit Wakeman, his father. The hollow echoes became louder, filling her head like the pealing of bells and the faces before her shifted and blurred. The kitchen floor tipped and Anne fell in a faint at her husband's feet.

It was providential that Goody Trewitt's nose could smell out food a mile away. In no time at all she was wafting a burned feather under Anne's nose to revive her and at the same time thanking all the saints in Christendom that John was back with his head still on his shoulders.

"What ails Anne? What have you said to upset her so?" she demanded.

"It was yonder document." John pointed to the deed that lay on the table. "Read it, Goody, then perhaps you can convince my Anne, for she will not believe what I tell her."

Goody glanced at the parchment, and sniffed. "I read only a little Latin. You must tell me what the words say.

Patiently John explained the significance of the deed and title. Goody listened calmly, slapping Anne's face and rubbing her hands as she did so.

"Come now, mistress, and open your eyes. 'Tis only your John come home with the Manor of Aldbridge in his pocket. 'Tis not the Day of Judgement."

Goody helped Anne to her feet.

" She is faint from lack of nourishment. You know, John, that yonder simple Polly eats enough to feed two babies whilst Anne goes hungry? What is to become of us all, I do not know."

" We will survive, Goody. I have money enough to sustain us all until we can gather in our crops again. Sit with us and share what there is, and welcome."

Goody spread bacon fat on her bread.

" Now tell us of your travels John. They say the Queen has black pearls the size of muscat grapes. Did you see her black pearls, John?"

" I did not!"

" Tell me then, what did she eat? They say she feasts on tongues of larks and strawberries dipped in wine and sugar, and eats marchpane the whole day long."

" I cannot tell you what she eats, for I did not sup with Her Grace. I remember there were oranges, though. When first I met the Queen there was a bowl of oranges on a table by her chair in her little private chamber."

" Was she beautiful, John?" Anne asked.

" Yes, beautiful, is she not Martin?"

Martin Hewitt nodded. Martin was a Londoner, and Londoners adored their Queen. Had she been a pock-marked hag, he would still have thought her beautiful.

John thought for a moment. " She is not just beautiful. She is golden. Can you understand? Her eyes, her hair, even the very air around her—all things about her person seemed touched by the sun."

Goody Trewitt belched with disbelief, and rubbed her plate with the last of her bread.

"Why did she not wear her black pearls?" she asked.

John laughed. "I don't know. The first time I saw her, the pearls she wore were milk white, almost as white as her hands." John looked at Anne's hands, red with scrubbing and rough from spinning, and took them in his own. "Her hands were almost as beautiful as yours, Anne."

"What of her gown, John? Was her gown beautiful?"

"Her gown was made of satin—green, like the colour of ash leaves at springtime, and embroidered in silver and black. And she wore pearls in her hair."

"John, I begin to believe you did see the Queen." Anne was still bemused. "Am I truly awake?"

"You are truly awake, dearest Anne. Will you believe that I saw the Queen not once, but twice?" John turned to his friend. "Did you not take me to the Palace of Westminster, Martin, and were we not commanded to return to the Queen's presence on the morrow?"

"That we were, Sir John. But women were ever doubtful. Your good lady would not believe you, were the Archbishop himself to swear it for you!"

"You went twice to the Queen, John? What business took you to the Court a second time?"

"Faith, I'll swear I did not know myself. I had an audience with Her Majesty. None were there save Lord Burghley and Mistress Ashley. The Queen asked about Meg and the babe, then thanked me for my loyalty. It seemed she was about to give me a purse of gold, but she did not. Suddenly I was commanded to return the following day at noon."

It was best, thought John, that he did not speak of the Queen's tantrum nor the purse of sovereigns that hurtled through the air. Some things were not spoken of by men of honour and that must always be one of them, or Goody would retail it to every housewife in the Riding, and eat well on it for many a week.

" And on that following day, did she wear her black pearls, big as muscat grapes?"

" Nay, Goody," said John. " On that day the Queen wore a bracelet at her wrist. It was set with rubies and diamonds, and know you there was a clock, a *tiny clock* set in its clasp? The clock was so dainty it would scarce have covered my thumbnail!"

John remembered about the clock and wondered what craftsman could have made one so small and perfect. He had seen the bracelet as he knelt before the Queen. She had worn it on her right wrist. He had noticed it especially, since that was the hand in which she had held the slender sword. He wished all his memories of that afternoon were as clear.

" John Weaver," the Queen had said, " your loyalty has pleased us, and we give to you the lands and title of the Manor of Aldbridge, commanding that you defend them for us, and for your issue, for all time."

John had not realised the significance of the tap of the sword on his shoulder.

" And now arise, Sir John!"

There was a murmur of polite applause from Elizabeth's Court as a leather purse was placed in his hand. It was foolish at such a time John knew, but he wondered if it had been Mistress Ashley who picked up the sovereigns.

" Come close, Sir John," the Queen beckoned. She looked at him for a moment and then slowly and quietly repeated the words she had said to him the day before. " Care well for Harry, your son, and guard well this, *his inheritance*." She placed the parchment in his hand. " God go with you, Sir John."

John's heart beat so loudly that he feared the whole court must hear it. Proudly he held his head high. This time he remembered what they had told him. Bowing carefully as he had seen the courtiers do, he took a step away from the Queen. " God bless your Grace," he whispered and bowed again, walking slowly and clumsily backwards until he was a discreet distance from her. He stood for a moment and looked at the golden Elizabeth before making his final homage.

The Queen inclined her head. She had given to his care the hundred souls of the village of Aldbridge, the lands and the dwelling houses, the mill and the smithy, four fair farmsteads, and the great Manor. All this was his to hold for Harry, Meg's love-child.

" What was in your mind when the Queen dubbed you knight? What thoughts go through a man's head at such a time?"

John rubbed his ear and smiled. " They were not the thoughts of a gentleman, Anne, that I must confess. I remember kneeling and seeing the Queen's dainty slippers, and know you, Anne, her stockings were of finest silk, and shaped to cling to her ankle? What fairy-fine needles they were knitted on I do not know, nor what craftsman had made them so, but they were the daintiest hose I ever did see, and the colour of saffron."

" Shame on you, John Weaver!" teased Martin. " Men have lost their heads for less!"

" I'll swear I meant no disrespect to Her Grace. 'Twas just that I have never seen such stockings! "

And still Anne could not believe her husband. Not even when he had given her the length of yellow satin he had bought in London's Royal Exchange, and the fine hat he had purchased in Cheapside. Anne was now a lady of title and must discard her knitted caps. The sight of the green bonnet with its proud yellow feather had done little to convince her of her new status.

" What must I do, Goody, to make my Anne realise what has come to pass? "

But such news as John's could not wait for the telling. Goody was off as fast as her fat legs would carry her to tell all and sundry of John Weaver's good fortune. And Queen Elizabeth's black pearls!

Some hours later, John looked down at his sleeping wife. The day had been one of strangeness for her and the growing awareness of her new status had been almost too much for her to accept. Now, with the help of a sleeping draught from Goody, she lay quiet.

Gently John smoothed her hair and pulled the blankets over her shoulders before he left the room. In the little garret where once Meg had slept lay buxom Polly, a smile of contentment on her simpleton face. Beside her in his wooden crib lay Meg's love-child, his cheeks fat and rosy, despite the near famine that lay over the North.

Quietly John stepped down the loft staircase. The kitchen was quiet now the excitement was over. Goody had gone, eager to be back to her tittle-tattling, and Martin had left for York, and the accommodating wench who would now be warming his bed. Only Father Sedgwick remained, sitting quietly by the fireside.

" Is all well? " he asked.

" Aye, Father. Anne sleeps quietly now. This day has been one she will remember for a long time. Even now, I think she does not fully understand its meaning."

" The babe thrives? "

" Aye, thank God, though how Anne has found sustenance for the wet-nurse, I do not know. I must away to market as soon as I can. The Queen gave me money and I will spend it on food for the villagers. They are in my charge now. Somehow I must provide for them until another harvest is gathered."

" You will do your duty, Sir John, that I know. None will begrudge you your new station in life." The priest stared at the floor. " You are a good man, John Weaver. It has often plagued me that my conscience would not let me give absolution to Meg before she died. The mortal sin I could have forgiven; 'twas the witchcraft that had me feared."

" The mortal sin? "

For a moment they faced each other, the priest wishing he could swallow his words, for he had not intended to say so much. Slowly the implication of the priest's words became clear. " You know about Meg's baby? I had not realised Father, that you knew the baby did not belong to Anne and myself."

" I guessed it, Sir John. Young Jeffrey came to my door and begged that I make haste for Meg was dying of the childbed. He was distressed, and did not know what he had said."

G

" You did not come, but held your peace. Why? "

" Must a man have a reason for everything he does? I can only tell you that if any man knows, he has not gained knowledge from me. What Jeffrey told me in a moment of anguish was treated as I would treat a man's confession. Mistress Trewitt had told me your wife was with child, and I accepted it. When I heard she had been delivered of a son, I held my tongue."

" Then I am in your debt, Father. I was sorely grieved that you would not baptise the child, and that Meg lies in unholy ground without the blessing of the Church, but for what you did, I am grateful. Will you keep our secret? "

" Who am I, Sir John, to gainsay the Queen? " Father Sedgwick was anxious for the safety of his good living. " She makes it pretty plain in the title deed that the child is legitimised."

John smiled. He would remember always the purse of sovereigns that shattered against the wall.

" Then the babe's secret is safe, for those who know are our trusted friends. I am grateful to you, Father Sedgwick for reading the document to my Anne. She would not believe what I told her. Will you do one more favour for me? "

" That I will Sir John, and gladly, if it is in my power."

" Then go with me to where Meg lies buried and give her absolution that she may rest. None know her grave, not even her mother. It is dark now, and no one will see us. Will you do it for an innocent maid? "

" I will do as you ask," he said, contritely.

TWENTY

THE STRANGE little procession halted by the open gates. Beyond them the Manor stood silent and neglected. The latticed panes in the mullion windows were unwashed and the dead leaves of winter lay rotting beneath the stone porch. The cattle John drove before him lumbered on, their hides stretched tight over skeletal frames, their tongues searching hungrily for the spring grass.

John remembered the last time he had visited the Manor, and wished he could forget it. For him, revenge had not been sweet. He saw before him not Harry's inheritance, but his own thirty pieces of silver. He and Anne were leaving the farmhouse where they had been so happy, and it seemed that they were leaving behind the sweet pale child who was once their daughter. But no matter where they travelled or how far, the unhappy little wraith would always be at John's side.

"Meg?" His lips formed her name as though to reassure himself she were still beside him as he entered the great house. He could not bear it if she became lost in surroundings that were strange to her. An impatient cluck from Anne called him from his day-dream.

" I'll swear, John, I have never seen such neglect. Lady Hilda would not have permitted it. There'll be a week's work here for half the village, or I'm sadly mistaken!"

Kicking aside her skirts she walked up the steps she had swept so often and pushed open the unlocked door.

" Lord's sake, John, what has happened?"

Before them lay the desolation and neglect of many months. No fire burned in the great hearth and dirt was everywhere. The room smelled stale and dank.

" Lady Hilda must have had the wind at her backside when she left," Goody Trewitt looked round the vast room with distaste. " I'll swear she fled with nothing but what she stood up in."

The long table was still laid with goblets and plates of food, and what the rats had not gnawed lay rotten and stinking. In the hearth where once huge logs had spat and crackled lay the remains of blackened parchment.

" Perhaps when we have lit fires and warmed the rooms it will seem more like home," suggested John hopefully.

" Will this place ever be home to us?" Anne reached out as she always did in times of stress, for her husband's hand. She was not ungrateful. She complained only to hide her true feelings. In her heart she was proud and glad for John's sake, and for Harry's too, that she should stand here now, lady of the manor where once she had worked as a servant. Perhaps in time she would not remember the old days so clearly.

Anne opened the door that led to the winter parlour. It had once been Lady Hilda's favourite room. She had sat there at her embroidery or instructed her servants in the art of sewing. Anne remembered those days well and the gaiety and chatter as they had all mended the household linen or repaired the heavy hangings or the vestments from the church. Lady Hilda had been a good and fair mistress and had taught her servants how a comfortable home should be run.

Anne knew she had much to thank her for. Perhaps some day she herself would sit in the cosy little room and chide her own servants for their clumsy stitching or praise them for their neat darns. It was all so strange, almost like beginning another life. If only she could have awakened to Meg's happy laughter, or hear John singing as he used to do, as he milked his cows. But Anne knew those precious days would never return.

She turned to Polly who stood wide-eyed and uncertain at the threshold of the room.

" Come, little wench. There is nothing to fear. This is where you live now. Soon it will be clean and bright as a new pin," she said, as she laid a comforting arm round the dejected shoulders.

Anne walked across the room, her feet echoing in the vast void of neglect. In the corner stood the door that led to the kitchens. There she knew she would get her breath back, for there she had worked so happily many years ago. Those great kitchens once rang with the laughter of half a dozen serving girls, and the bustle of Feast Days and the merriment of Christmas had once been a part of Anne's life.

She stood quite still on the threshold, a strange tightness gripping her throat.

The spit was stuck with uncooked meat, now abandoned, and cold hard grease lay over the fireirons and cooking pots. Bread moulded on the table and rushes rotted on the floor. No red-faced spitboy stood sweating by the fire. No serving maid whisked her short skirts around the table and plagued the cook with her pert tongue. Pewter plates lay uncleaned and tables stood unscrubbed.

Tears threatened, and Anne squeezed her eyelids tight so they might not escape. She could not believe the strange desolation she saw before her. Once this house had seemed so safe and strong. Now it was a stinking neglected hulk of a place, rat infested, and quiet as a tomb.

The manor had been her other home. What had happened to it? What had happened, thought Anne, to her whole life? For a moment she stood fighting the hurt inside her, wondering what Lady Hilda would have made of it all. But Lady Hilda was gone now and she, Anne Weaver was in charge of this great house.

" Mistress Trewitt, if you know of two good wenches with strong arms, I'd be mortal glad of their services!"

Flinging her cloak on to the litter of the table, she rolled up her sleeves. First, a fire in the hearth, and then hot water and whisps of straw for scrubbing. By nightfall, even Lady Hilda would not be able to fault the kitchens should she return to inspect them.

Together, John and Jeffrey closed the stable doors. The livestock was bedded down and what hay could be found had been fed to them.

" I am grateful for your help today, Jeffrey. Will you return tomorrow and travel with me to market? I must buy what food I can, for everyone hereabouts starves. Soon your mill wheels will turn again when we have crops to harvest and grain to grind."

They walked to the great oak gates, and pulled them shut.

"Bid you goodnight, Sir John," Jeffrey said, and tipped his cap.

John stood for a moment and watched him walk towards the mill. Jeffrey had his widowed mother and young brother to provide for, but at least they had their home back. If only Meg had married Jeffrey. But she had not married him. Meg was dead and she had called for Kit Wakeman with her last breath. Now, too, Kit was dead. Had Kit called for Meg, and had Meg heard him? Meg believed in her innocence that she could come again. Had she not said as she died that one day she would find Kit? Could he, thought John, keep the pale little ghost by his side, or was she eager to be away to search for her love? John turned to the house that was now his own.

"Your home is here, Meg. You live here, now," he whispered. "Stay with me, little bird."

But John knew that one day he must sever the bonds of love that tied Meg to him. She belonged with Kit, and soon he knew he must release her.

John looked up to where Sir Crispin Wakeman's arms had been chiseled into the stone above the massive doors. Some day he must ask for a coat of arms for young Harry. He wondered what a humble weaver could pass on that might be emblazoned on a family crest.

The door creaked open, and Anne stood there.

"John, are you star-gazing? The small parlour is cleaned and warm and supper is ready. Come, and eat what food there is."

" Aye, Anne, but first tell me of what devices we shall make our crest when the time comes. We cannot take Sir Crispin's arms for our own. What do you think the Weavers should adopt for their crest?"

" I know not." Anne spoke with impatience. " And at this moment I care not!"

John held out his hand to her. " Stay with me a while. You are right. It does not matter at this moment, but one day it will be of importance to young Harry. What would you give him for his coat of arms?"

" The shuttle of a weaver," the forthright Anne declared, " that he might be proud of his beginnings."

" And for Elizabeth Tudor who gave it to him? What would we put there for her?"

Anne thought for a moment. " Did you not call her your golden Queen? What more golden than a sheaf of wheat grown on the beautiful plain of York?"

John laughed with delight. " A shuttle and a wheat-sheaf! And for York, the rose?"

" Yes," nodded Anne. " Was not Elizabeth of York the grandmother of your golden Elizabeth, and was not the white rose her emblem?"

Then they were silent, for they felt the gentle ghost that stood between them, and knew she could not join in their laughter.

" And for Meg?" asked Anne.

" For Meg we will tangle a flower with York's white rose," John replied softly. " For Meg I choose a heartsease, and forever I will see her face in every wild pansy that grows."

Together they walked to the warmth of the fire.

" Yes Anne, that is good. A heartsease for Meg."

By the stone-pit at the crossroads, John Weaver addressed the villagers of Aldbridge, on the following forenoon.

" Good people, I have called you to this spot that you may hear what I have to tell you."

He looked at the dejected huddle of men and women who stood around him, their eyes blank in hungry faces, their shoulders stooping for lack of pride that might have lifted them. They did not know why they had been summoned to the old stone-pit, instead of the church or the green, but they did not care to ask why.

They had suffered horribly during the months that had followed the uprising. Some of the men who stood by the crossroads that day had marched hopefully behind Sir Crispin to war, despite their natural Yorkshire caution. It might have been better by far if they had not returned. Of those who were missing from their homes, none knew whether they lay dead or unshriven, or whether they had fled over the borders into the Scottish Marches to the shelter of lairds who were known sympathisers of Mary Stuart.

It seemed strange to John that despite the charge of complicity to murder that hung over her, and John Knox's Puritanical rantings about her whoring with the Earl of Bothwell, Mary had her fanatical followers still. It seemed stranger still that she, the cause of the suffering was alive and well under Elizabeth Tudor's protection.

John's heart went out in pity to the innocents who stood there that day, for though they had had no part in the rebellion they had seen their cattle driven off or slaughtered and their belongings burned. The pathetic few bags of grain the troopers had found in lifts and barns had been taken away or callously destroyed.

And still on Gibbet Hill swayed the bodies of Jeffrey's father and brother with wind tattered clothing clinging to their putrefying flesh. It was wrong, thought John, that they should hang there until they dropped. Now when the gaunt old tree looked less forbidding with its tender veil of green spring buds, would be a good time to release them from the ridicule of passers-by and the derisive spittle of bitter widows.

Father Sedgwick must give them absolution, and lay them decently in the earth. However wrong they had been and however much suffering their actions had caused, they deserved the dignity of Christian burial. None knew that better than John himself.

The stamping of cold feet jerked John from his far-away thoughts. Few men now had boots. Those who had killed their cattle had tanned their leather and were lucky. But mostly the frost-bitten feet of winter were wrapped round in rags, and tied secure with thongs of leather.

" Good friends," continued John, his voice rough with emotion, " I am returned from London, charged by Elizabeth Tudor with the care of the Manor and lands of Aldbridge. Father Sedgwick," John nodded to the priest who stood by his side, " will vouch for the deed of title I carried home with me. Times are hard, and food is scarce, I have money given by our Queen and it will provide for your needs until we harvest our crops again."

There was a murmur of approval from the by-standers. It mattered little to them who lived at the Manor. Their bellies were empty and John Weaver had promised them food. It was all they cared to know. And God bless Queen Elizabeth for her bounty!

" It will be hard for a time for us all, but what I have I will share with you. At all times I will aid you if it is in my power, and until better days shall come, I will ask neither rents nor tithes from any man. Lady Anne," proudly John took his wife's hand, " will be glad to help you also if you have any problems that plague you."

Anne inclined her head as she had so often seen Lady Hilda do. The bright green feather in her hat nodded proudly, confirming her fine new status. She did not speak, for if she did she knew the tears would flow unchecked, and this must not happen. Lady Hilda had never wept in public.

" And now good friends, I give you a promise." John lifted the sapling oak he had carefully dug from the garden at the farm before they left. " This oak, I hold, I plant as a token. May it grow in strength, for as long as it grows will the name of Weaver flourish amongst you, and protect all honest souls in this village. Whilst this oak lives, I swear there will be a Weaver at the Manor and one who will love and care for you as his bounden duty. And further I tell you that the child Harry who was given to us late in our years, will learn from his cradle to serve and love you all as I do."

John walked to the scattering of stones and carefully and tenderly moved them, and taking the spade that Jeffrey carried, he gently removed the first sod.

" Now, good Jeffrey, will you plant my sapling at this very spot? Plant it with care and plant it well that it may grow straight and true."

Proudly Jeffrey drove the stave he carried into the earth beside the tree, carefully tying it for support. Firmly he pressed down the earth round the tree, with his foot, and as he did so, John saw the flowers.

" Hold, Jeffrey! "

At first he could not believe what he saw, for it was unexpected as it was uncanny. Growing in the earth that clung to the roots of the sapling oak was a clump of hearts-ease, and flowering bravely, long before their season. Their tiny faces were turned up to him, and in their innocence John was reminded of Meg. It is a sign, thought John, his heart pumping wildly.

" Have a care, Jeffrey. Do not tread on the heartsease! "

John fell to his knees and gently pressed the little plant more firmly into the earth at the base of the young tree.

" Stand not on a heartsease . . ." he whispered, almost inaudibly.

John's mouth felt dry, and his hands trembled with excitement. Truly, he repeated to himself, the flowers *must* be a sign, for never before had he seen a heartsease flower at a time of the year when only the snowdrops were nodding their heads. The small brave pansies were more than a sign; they were a little miracle.

Last night, as John had stood with Father Sedgwick at this same spot, there had been a faint sad cry as the priest had raised his hand in absolution over Meg's grave. Perhaps it had been the night cry of a plover. " Pee-wit! Pee-wit! " Plovers were sad, lonely birds. They often cried in the darkness.

But could that call have been something else? thought John. Could a pale little soul have called into the night, crying for her lover? Had that soul been Meg's soul and had she called out "Kit! Kit!" Had it been a sign like the heartsease that clung to the sapling, blooming before their time? *What are you trying to tell me, Meg?* John begged, silently.

Slowly he rose to his feet, aware of the curious stares round him. How long he knelt there, he did not know.

" Away now to your homes, good people. Take care of this oak, and let no one molest it, so that we all may flourish!"

Father Sedgwick lifted his hand and blessed the little tree, and the ground into which it had been planted . . .

The crossroads, deserted now but for Anne and John, was quiet once more. For a while neither of them spoke, then Anne reached out with her hand to find John's.

" You planted well, husband," she said, softly, gazing at the little tree. " Now none will disturb Meg's resting place, for none will dare disturb John Weaver's oak!"

She looked at him, happiness shining in her eyes.

For a while John could not trust himself to speak, then glad beyond measure that at last she knew, he gathered her into his arms.

For a second in time all was so still that John could feel and hear the silence all about him. Then, from the topmost branches of a nearby tree, a bird piped out its first song of spring. For one sweet moment the months rolled away and a blackbird in an apple tree sang again in a soft July twilight.

John knew he could not keep Meg. He must release her, for she did not belong to him. Somewhere Kit was waiting for her, and she must find him. Her freedom was all he could give to her now.

" Meg, little wench," whispered John, " he is waiting for you. Go with my love. Go to your Kit, little heart, and be happy."

Gently Anne's fingers tightened round John's.

" And you, dear husband, come back to your Anne. You have been away so long in a world of misery. The nightmare is over."

John took the hand that enfolded his and held it to his cheek, the feeling of happiness suffocating him so that he could hardly speak. Then lifting the dear familiar hand to his lips, he softly kissed its palm.

" I do love you, my Lady Weaver," he whispered. " I do so love you."